Iza Duffus Hardy

A Hero's Work

Volume 2

Iza Duffus Hardy

A Hero's Work
Volume 2

ISBN/EAN: 9783337195984

Printed in Europe, USA, Canada, Australia, Japan

Cover: Foto ©Andreas Hilbeck / pixelio.de

More available books at **www.hansebooks.com**

A HERO'S WORK

BY

MRS. DUFFUS HARDY,

AUTHOR OF

"A CASUAL ACQUAINTANCE,"

&c., &c.

IN THREE VOLUMES.

VOL. II.

LONDON:

HURST AND BLACKETT, PUBLISHERS,

13, GREAT MARLBOROUGH STREET.

1868.

The right of Translation is reserved.

LONDON:
PRINTED BY MACDONALD AND TUGWELL,
BLENHEIM HOUSE.

CHAPTER I.

A NEW LIGHT.

"I give thee all! I can no more—
Though poor the offering be."

DAYS rolled on, and Adrienne slowly re-covered, thanks to the unremitting care of Mr. Sterndale. Before the autumn leaves had fallen, she had resumed her former solitary life, with her old faithful companion, Neptune; the two were rarely, if ever, seen apart—they went wandering over the grounds, or about the garden in lonely companionship; the dog, it must be owned, looking wiser and graver than his young mistress, whose spirits were untamed by her sharp suffering—indeed, at times, they seemed to have become more reckless and daring than before. The sick-room had been any-thing but a school of repentance to her; she had learned nothing there, not even to regret. Her folly had been held so constantly before her eyes, painted in such fierce, fiery characters, so ex-aggerated and enlarged, that, instead of repent-ing, she had learned to laugh at it. Sometimes, even in her mother's hearing, she would, in a wild rambling fashion, talk the matter over with "Nep," and, as the creature wagged his tail, looking at her with his wise brown eyes, she would declare that he not only understood, but approved of, every word she uttered.

"How we enjoyed that scamper over the hills, you and I, didn't we, Nep? Look, Ma-thilde, when he wags his tail three times, it means 'yes.' But we were very naughty, Nep, were we not? It was forbidden fruit—heigho! for all that, we should like another bite of it, shouldn't we, Nep? I am afraid, if you had been Adam, and I had been Eve, we should have eaten up the whole tree, root and branch."

In vain Mathilde looked at her sister with imploring eyes, as though beseeching her to be silent ; Adrienne heeded her not, but rattled on the more, until her mother, losing all patience, silenced her with some pungent and well-deserved rebuke, which she dared not, or could not answer. Mathilde, as soon as they were alone, expostulated with her.

"Why will you be so foolish, Adrienne?" she said, one day; "how wrong it is to irritate mamma, when you know it can do no possible good!"

"It does *me* a great deal of good," said Adrienne; "it proves that, if I cannot win her love, I can at least rouse her anger; that's something. I know it is gall and bitterness to her, to see that I can be happy, in spite of her. She does her best to crush me, body and soul; thank Heaven! she has not the power. Oh! Mathilde, sister darling, why does my mother hate me?"

In this passionate cry which burst from her

heart, there spoke the young girl's yearning for a mother's love and sympathy, which her wilful and rebellious words denied.

"She does not hate you, Adrienne," said Mathilde; "but your natures are so opposite. You are wayward, she is exacting. If there is any yielding, and yielding there must be, if you would have peace, it should be by you, Adrienne; children owe some duty to their parents."

"Yes, but parents also owe some duty to their children. If they fail in theirs, it is no wonder that we fail in ours. We are brought into this world, poor, helpless, unconscious beings, and it is our parent's duty to guide and direct us—to sweeten the life they have given, not embitter it. My life has been a continued course of petty tyrannies. Oh! Mathilde, I am ashamed to own how much they have oppressed me, wounded me to the heart's core. I feel I have a right to rebel, and I do rebel, with my whole heart and soul, against my mother's authority, for it is ill-used; but, thank God!"

she added, with a deep-drawn breath, "it cannot last for ever—one day I shall be free."

"Oh! Adrienne," said her sister, earnestly, "I think I know, in part, what vexes, what has always vexed, our mother's heart. It is not that she loves you less than she loves me, but that she has less authority over you."

"Less authority? What do you mean?" exclaimed Adrienne, with a puzzled air. "At any rate, if she has but little, she makes that little go a great way."

"I mean," added Mathilde, "that by your father's will, you are left independent of her when you are of age. You will inherit all, or nearly all, his property, without her control; you will then be your own mistress, with a large fortune at command. I know she does not like to feel that, when your girlhood is past, her influence over you will be gone."

"It is a mother's own fault if her influence ever fails," replied Adrienne. "She might have made me what she pleased, if she had gone the right way to work, instead of the wrong. If she had ever loved, or cared for me, I should have paid her back with tenfold interest."

"There is another cause that disunites, and keeps you wide asunder," said Mathilde, regretfully. "You have been brought up in a different faith, the one cannot sympathise with the other; there is no religious bond of union between you. Then, again, you have a most unruly tongue, Adrienne, you are so full of mockeries and irony."

"I cannot help it; my tongue is the only weapon that I can use in self-defence. When I am stung, I can sting again with that. There, Mathilde, it is no use talking, there are times when I cannot control myself. I must speak, even if I knew I should be killed the next minute!"

"But remember, Adrienne, for every gibing, impulsive word you speak you suffer tenfold."

"I do not care for that," answered the wilful

girl, "there is nothing like tyranny for giving pains and heartburn. *You,* my poor angel sister," she added, caressingly, "bear anything, but I cannot—when I am tried too far, I retort, and when mamma fixes on me her cold, bitter eyes, I am glad—then I know she hates me, and would like to see me dead, yet she dares not kill me. Oh! it is hard, very hard, to be so hated by one's own mother! No one cares for me, no one in the world but you, dear, dear Mathilde!" and she threw herself sobbing in her sister's arms.

"My darling Adrienne! my own bright one!" the crippled girl answered, caressing her fondly, and letting her own tears fall like rain-drops over her, "you are the comfort and blessing of my life; it breaks my heart to see you and mamma so constantly at variance, to know that you are unhappy, and to feel that I can do nothing to save you from a single pang, nothing but pray for you. Sister, darling," she whispered, "for my sake, for your own soul's sake, try to bear and forbear; it may be hard at first, but it will come easier by-and-bye—remember that, at every harsh word you crush upon you lips, angels rejoice in heaven, and God himself looks down and smiles upon you!"

For some days after this conversation, Adrienne put on her best behaviour. A look from her afflicted sister quelled the rising wrath that was ever ready to gush forth in saucy words. Her warm, impulsive nature could be controlled and guided utterly by love; but it rose up, armed at every point, against injustice. Upon Adrienne's changed behaviour, Madame de Fontaine relaxed very much in her severities; she permitted her more liberty, and occasionally allowed her to spend a whole day at the Rectory. These were bright, happy times for Adrienne; perhaps the happiest she had ever known. A cheerful welcome, from warm hearts and smiling faces, always awaited her at the Carltons'; they made her quite at home, and received her as one of the family. The intimacy quickly arrived at that stage when it was no longer necessary to ring the bell for admission; she, Nep as *avant-courrier*, would cross the lawn and enter the house through the French windows, which were generally left open during the fine autumn days. If she could not find some of the family in one room, she wandered on to another, or stationed herself at the foot of the stairs, or under the windows, and warbled with her sweet, melodious voice one of those French songs of Béranger's, which she had learned to know they loved. Long before the song was ended, she was sure to receive an affectionate embrace or hearty greeting from some one member of the family. It was delightful to her to feel that she never arrived at an inconvenient time, never was unwelcome.

Nep was almost as much at home at the Rectory as his young mistress; so soon as the Manor-house gates were open, he knew which way to go, and started off in the direction of the Rectory. If Adrienne had made an appointment with the Carltons, and anything happened to prevent her keeping it, she would write a letter, and shake it in Nep's face till he blinked his brown eyes, and seemed to understand all about it; then she attached it to his collar, and sent him off to the Rectory, whither he went direct, and delivered his *billet*, like a trusty messenger as he was. Woe be to anyone who attempted to interfere with him, or meddle with that which his mistress had entrusted to his care.

One day Madame de Fontaine, ever on the watch, ever suspicious of Adrienne, or Adrienne's friends, intercepted him as he was gravely making his way across the meadows to the Rectory. He listened respectfully, though with a leer of suspicion in his wise eyes, as she patted and petted him, calling him "good dog," "pretty Nep;" but when her hands crept softly near and nearer to his neck, he showed his teeth. Undaunted at his threat, she laid hold of his collar, and in a second would have secured the note; but Nep, with a sharp, quick growl, turned his head, left his mark upon her hand, and tore away across the fields. She rose from her stooping posture, black with rage; her eyes positively glared as she glanced after the animal bounding away in the distance. She looked down at her hurt—it was a mere scratch, but a thin streak of blood was oozing slowly from it. She covered it quickly, and turned her steps homeward—she had never liked the dog, now she hated it. She kept her hand covered as much as possible during the day; but in spite of all her care, Adrienne's sharp eyes discovered what her mother was so anxious to hide.

"Why, mamma, what is the matter with your hand?" she exclaimed; "it looks as though it had been bleeding."

"It is nothing," replied her mother, hastily covering the wound. After a moment's pause she added quietly, "Your dog is getting too savage for a reasonable family; he must be got rid of."

"Did Nep do that?" exclaimed Adrienne, un-heeding, in her concern for her mother's injury, the threat contained in the last sentence. "Oh! mamma, I am so sorry—how could it have happened? Nep is the gentlest, noblest, dearest beast in all the world."

"As a proof of his gentleness, I shall carry a scar to my grave," replied Madame de Fontaine; "but no matter—I know he has always been your dear friend and companion, now he has tasted your mother's blood, he may be dearer still."

Adrienne was deeply distressed at what had happened; she bore her mother's unjust insinuation meekly; and though hurt by the cruel words, she made no attempt to reply. She felt that her mother had some cause of complaint, and was ready to make every allowance for her wrath against herself; though she could not but think that her mother had given Nep grave cause of offence, she knew that she was not likely to hear the true story.

In due time Neptune returned, with drooping tail and ears laid back ; there was a guilty look in his face, as he listened gravely to Adrienne's reproaches, and a wistful look in his eyes, as though he would fain have pleaded his own cause, but could not.

In all Adrienne's visits to the Rectory, she never once caught a glimpse of the skeleton that haunted it, in the shape of Laurence Carlton, that restless, discontented inhabitant of the paternal mansion. His relations with his father were by no means improved with time. At the end of two or three months there was no more cordiality between them than had existed at the beginning of his visit. The young man felt that he was an eyesore in his father's sight, and kept out of it as much as possible. For days together they did not exchange a word—indeed, they met as seldom as possible. The father was anxious, full of trouble, and sad absorbing thoughts for the future ; the son, irritable and harassed with the reflection that he had deserved to lose his father's confidence; and however much in his heart he desired to regain it, he made no outward sign, but went on his way in moody silence, spending his hours, often his days, in questionable company at the "Grapes Inn." Mrs. Carlton knew that things could not go on in this way for ever. Again she suggested to her husband that he should let Laurence have another trial—give him one more start in the world, and allow him to choose for himself the direction in which that start should be.

"I have tried him too often, Christina," answered the Rector, gravely; "he will never do any good. What will become of him Heaven only knows—I do not. It is very hard, and he my only son, too, but it cannot be helped; there must be some wise purpose, so I will not complain. If he will not work like a man, he must live at home dependent as a girl."

"But he cannot live a life as innocent as a

girl's," replied Mrs. Carlton; "it is not in man's nature, Edward. If he is not doing good, be sure he is doing evil. You must know that the life he is leading now can bring no credit either to himself or to you."

"I know it well," said the Rector, helplessly; "but what can I do? He is rebellious and self-willed; I have no longer, as a father, any authority over him."

"No," replied Mrs. Carlton, "perhaps not; but though you can no longer rule him as a father, yet you may still influence him as a man. You must give him one more trial, Edward. Come, promise me that you will," she added, looking pleadingly in his face—"indeed you must. I will take no denial; I will not consent to be only half a mother to your children; I will have a mother's whole rights or none; and one of the best and holiest, Edward, is to bring peace where there has been strife."

"You are all goodness to them and to me,"

replied Mr. Carlton, smiling fondly, as he drew his wife closer to his side, and kissed her smooth fair cheek.

The old love-light was still burning bright and strong in his heart; it had never been quenched, though a flood of sorrow had rolled heavily over it. Grave, grey-haired man as he was, it leaped up now, and gleamed out with a warm steady glow from his eyes, as he looked upon his wife's face. The flickering passion of youth had burnt itself out long ago, but in its place the love of the man had grown full and strong. For twenty years and more she had stood like a shrined saint in the halls of his memory. In the hour of need, when, deprived of his first wife, he stood alone, perplexed with the tangled business of the world, she had stepped out from the gloomy past, and brightened the present with the hope of the future, by taking her place by his side as the companion of his soul, and the mother of his motherless children. He was not a demonstrative man, but, in his

thoughtful mind, he surrounded her with all
the poetry of his nature. He felt deeply her
unvarying affection to his children; he well
knew those circumstances which, in a meaner
soul than hers, might have operated against
them. When she pleaded for his graceless son,
though there was not much in his words as he
answered, there was a great deal in his tone
and his look as he repeated again—

"You are all goodness to them and to me—
I will think the matter over by-and-bye."

"No, no," she answered, "I will not let you
off so—think it over, indeed!—it needs no
thought; act at once. Send for Laurence, open
your heart to him, talk to him, not as father
to son, but as man to man; tell him what you
will, what you can do, and let him choose for
himself. He has a good heart, and plenty of
common sense; it requires only to be turned in
the right direction. Come, you must see him
and make your arrangements at once."

"Not to-day, I cannot."

"Why?"

"You remember I am going to London. I have several little matters of business to attend to; besides, the winter is approaching, and I want money to make small purchases for my poor parishioners. I want to sell out, and place a larger balance in my county banker's hands, for I don't want to go up to town again for some time. You know," he added, "I can't give a poor woman a check for a loaf of bread."

"Who's that?" exclaimed Mrs. Carlton quickly, as she saw a shadow pass suddenly across the grass. In a second she was out upon the lawn, making towards a rough, stupid-looking fellow, who at her approach pulled a ragged cap from his head, and took out a letter, which he said he had brought for young Squire Carlton.

"You should have rung the bell, and the servants would have received any message you may have for my son," replied the Rector, sternly, who had joined his wife. "I don't allow strangers to sneak into my private grounds, and peer in at my open windows like a thief in the night. You may be an honest man, though your mode of entrance subjects you to the suspicion of being a rogue and a vagabond."

The man, who really looked too stupid to understand the rebuke, muttered something about "being a stranger in these parts, and not knowing the ways o' the gentry."

"From whom is the letter?" inquired Mr. Carlton. "Are you to wait for an answer?"

"It's from a gennelman at the 'Grapes,' as have come down from Lonnon last night, and I dunnow if I'm to wait for a answer or not—wasn't told," replied the man surlily.

"Give me the letter," said the Rector, stretching out his hand to receive it; "my son is from home. It shall be delivered to him as soon as he returns."

With evident reluctance the man placed the letter in the Rector's outstretched hand. Saying, "I dosn't know as how I do right, though, in giving it you," he shambled his way out of the garden, evidently glad to get away from the Rector's scrutiny.

"I don't like the look of that man," said Mr. Carlton, gazing after his retreating figure; "I believe the fellow was eavesdropping, and heard every word we said."

"Very likely. But it does not much matter," said Mrs. Carlton, soothingly; she did not like to see her husband vexed; "we must have a gate put up at the end of the walk there, and prevent such intrusions for the future."

"Yes," replied the Rector, abstractedly, as though he were thinking of something else. After a moment's pause he added, abruptly, "You are quite right, Christina; something must be done with Laurence, or for him. I will see about it as soon as I come home."

"It is almost time you were gone," said Mrs. Carlton, looking at her watch; "it is now twelve o'clock, and the train starts at half-past one. There is just time to have some luncheon, then I will drive with you to the station."

At the appointed hour the little pony-carriage was brought to the door, and Mr. and Mrs. Carlton prepared for a pleasant drive through the green shady lanes, to the primitive station that stood in the rural district, about two miles on the other side of Crofton. The girls gave their father a folio sheet filled with all sorts of commissions, which he was expected to execute. He was threatened with the direst vengeance, to go unkissed and unloved for a week, if he dared to forget even one. They stood out in the rich sunshine, pouring their requirements and reminders into his ear until the last.

"Be sure you remember the musical-box—and my books, papa!" exclaimed Lena.

"And—oh! mind you don't forget a very handsome collar for Adrienne's dog," chimed in Grace; "brass-bound, with red leather—I've written everything down."

"Come, Edward, or you will be late," urged Mrs. Carlton, as the girls insisted on another hearty embrace before he started.

"Be sure you give your brother his letter the moment he comes home," were the last words the Rector uttered as he drove away. His daughters watched them till the carriage appeared like a speck in the distance.

About half an hour after their departure, Laurence moodily crossed the meadows, entered the house, went direct to his room, and locked himself in. As soon as Lena heard that he had returned, she went up to his room and tapped lightly at the door.

"Who's there?" he said. His voice sounded strangely gruff to Lena's ears, for he was always especially gentle and considerate to his sisters.

"It is I—Lena," she answered, rapping again impatiently; "open the door, Laurie."

"I cannot—I'm busy."

"But you must, I have a letter for you."

The door was opened in a moment, and Laurence eagerly held out his hand to receive the letter. He glanced at the superscription, tore open the envelope, and read it. He seemed greatly disturbed by its contents. A blank despairing look clouded his face. He crushed the letter in his hand, and thrust in into his vest, muttering between his clenched teeth some wild, terrible words. Lena stood watching him in silent amazement. She wondered if the letter had come from that dreadful-looking man whose presence had so discomposed her brother once before. Laurence neither heeded nor spoke to her. He was not indeed conscious that she stood there watching him, as he folded his arms, and strode about in his room; his eyes were cast moodily on the ground, his lips occasionally moving, but uttering no sound. At length she stopped him in his excited walk, and laid her hand upon his arm, saying,

"I see you are in trouble, Laurie. Can I do anything for you?"

"No—nothing. I forgot you were here, Lena. Go, there's a good girl, and leave me to myself."

"I cannot go and leave you like this, Laurie, don't ask me. If we were in any trouble, we should confide in you. We tell *you* everything. Why should you conceal your trouble from us?"

"Because you can do me no good," he answered.

"How can you know that, until you have told us what your trouble is?" said Lena. "Is it money you want?—if you do, I have some. I have not spent half my last quarter's allowance yet," she added quickly.

"My darling sister, my dear, good little Lena," he said, drawing her affectionately towards him, "no—your store of wealth would be to my wants like a drop of water in the ocean. If you will leave me to myself, Lena, I may perhaps be able to think over some way of arranging my affairs without troubling anybody."

Lena saw that he was in earnest about wishing her to go, and accordingly she went.

In about half an hour she returned to his room. He was there still, but no longer pacing to and fro with excited strides. He was sitting at the table in an attitude of deep despondency, his head drooping upon his breast. As she opened the door, he turned round and showed a face ashy pale; yet he tried to smile.

"Well, Lena, what is it now?—another *billet-doux*, eh? No?" he added, as she shook her head. On glancing down, he saw that she had something covered over with her silk apron. "Why, how mysterious you look, darling! What have you there?—a sick kitten, or a chicken with the pip?—I suppose you expect me to cure it."

"No, indeed," she answered; "but I have brought something which I hope will help to cure you." So saying, she placed a chair close to his, sat down, uncovered a small wooden box, which she held concealed, and drawing forth one by one her shining store of trinkets, laid them on the table. "I have not quite three pounds in money, Laurie," she added; "but look here, I should think you might get almost twenty pounds for these; and—ah! I forgot, there is my watch and chain—I seldom wear it; sometimes I forget to wind it up, and it remains for days together in its case, so it will never be missed." Laurence did not speak. After a moment's pause she added, "You need not mind taking them, Laurie, nobody will ever know it; they are mine, and I have a right to do what I please with them. Besides, papa never notices these things; and mamma says young girls look much better without trinkets."

Lena watched him anxiously; she saw by the working of his countenance that he was much moved. He took up the trinkets and examined them separately; a tender smile broke over his face, as he laid them down gently one by one. His eye rested a long time, with a musing, thoughtful look, upon a small Maltese cross, suspended by a thin gold chain. His lip trembled slightly, as though he had some difficulty in controlling his feelings; he held the ornament lightly on his finger as he said,

"Do you remember when you first wore this cross, Lena?"

"Yes; it was on my ninth birthday. Mamma gave it me; and I recollect another thing," she added smiling, "when I had once got it on, I would not take it off again, but I insisted on sleeping in it."

"I remember how you came dancing across the lawn to meet me, and to show me your little bit of finery," he added dreamily. "I fancy I can see you now. My mother stood watching at the window—God bless her! I am glad she is in her grave! You came *then* to gladden my eyes with this pretty toy, Lena; and *now* you bring it to cheer and relieve my heart."

"Oh! if they really will relieve you, I shall

be so happy!" exclaimed Lena, delighted at what she believed to be his ready acceptance of her simple offering. She gathered them together in a little heap and pushed them towards him; she took out her portmonnaie and emptied its contents upon the table—there were two sovereigns and some half-crowns and shillings in silver.

"Dear me!" she added, laughing, "I am richer than I thought. You had no idea your sister was such a woman of property. But it is all yours now—there, take it. I am going away."

He had watched her movements with moistening eyes, as she chatted and rattled the silver, gold, and trinkets together. As she pushed them towards him, he gently put them back.

"No, keep your poor little treasures, dear Lena. I would not rob you even of one."

"Rob me!" repeatedly Lena, disappointedly. "Oh! Laurie, how can you say anything so unkind! I ask you—I beg you to take them."

"No," he answered, and as he spoke his voice

had a choking, husky sound; "these are all, or nearly all, my dead mother's gifts—more than one I have seen her wear. Do you think that I would take what her hands have touched— her memory sanctified, to free myself from the dirty clutches of a usurer! No, I could not. Take them away. I would not use them even to save my life!"

"But, Laurie—" began his sister.

"But, Lena," he said, as with a melancholy smile he took her face between his hands, and kissed her forehead tenderly; "apart from all other feelings, scapegrace as I am, I would not put my pure little sister's treasures to so vile a use as to wipe out my disgraceful debts."

"They could not be put to a better," answered Lena.

"I know I am no genius," he continued, "and I may be but a brainless idiot; but I think I have got a heart somewhere, and you have touched it, Lena—touched it to the quick." He paused a moment, then added, "You know the black pool down in the wood? Well, rather than take advantage of your generous sisterly affection, I would lie down and take my last rest stark and stiff at the bottom of that slimy bed! Thank God, amid all my follies, I have not quite lost the spirit of a man!"

He sat down, and turned away his head, as though ashamed to show how much he was moved. Lena crept to his side, slipped her hand in his, and tried to rouse him by its soft warm pressure. They were both silent for a time; presently she whispered,

"Must things be always so, brother?"

"No," he answered, raising his face, now flushed with a sudden hope—a strong resolution; "with God's blessing, Lena, they shall *not* be always so. Let me once drift over my present difficulties, and I will not be found in muddled streams again. Sink or swim, I'll try the world once more; but I'll try it in my own fashion, Lena."

"First speak to papa, Laurie. I am sure he

will do anything for you, if you only give him your promise."

"I have given him so many already, Lena, and have never redeemed even one," answered Laurence. "No, no, deeds, not words, shall be my motto for the future; but—hark!" he raised his finger and listened breathlessly, as Adrienne's rich voice was heard in the garden, singing what she knew to be a favourite song at the Rectory, "Parlez nous de lui, Grand'mère."

"It is only Adrienne—do come down and see her," said Lena.

"Thank you, no," answered Laurence; "I am in no mood to play the agreeable to a young lady."

"I wish you would," urged Lena; "I am sure you would like her."

"Perhaps too well," he answered; "it is better to shun danger. I might fall a victim to an incurable complaint."

"And how I should rejoice to see you suffering!" exclaimed Lena. "It is just what I should like, above all things. Do you know, Laurie," she added, seriously, "I have often wished that you would fall in love with Adrienne, and she with you."

"Wish no such evil to your friend, if you love her, Lena," said Laurence, earnestly. "Come, trot off, or you will keep her waiting. Stay a minute, though," he added, as he turned back to the table, and carefully replaced her trinkets in the box. "Carry these away with you, Lena, dear; I can't say much now, but you will never know how much in my heart I thank you. You have administered a powerful tonic to my moral constitution, which was getting very feeble, Lena; but I think I shall recover, and be a whole strong man one day."

There was a world of grateful love in the bright glance he cast upon his sister's face as he opened the door for her to pass out. Laurence remained in his room some time after Lena had left him. His countenance reassumed a gloomy, thoughtful expression as he pondered over the letter which Lena had delivered to him. He was evidently in a sore strait, and stood alone in his trouble, aloof from all sympathy. He could make no confidantes in his own home, where only he might have obtained relief, for he would not intrude his sinful sorrow into that pure and honourable household. He concealed his self-inflicted wound from the physician who could have cured it, because he dreaded the knife that must probe, the hand that must cauterize, before it could heal. He knew he had richly deserved his father's severest censure, yet, with the inconsistency in human nature, he shrank from it with a sense of injury. He had spilt the oil of life at every step, and did not like to look back and see how much he had wasted, nor to look forward and see how little there was left.

As he sat there pondering, he heard the young girls flitting about the house, blending their voices together with familiar pleasantry;

their dresses rustled against his door as they passed by. He watched their light figures as they paced to and fro in the garden among the flower-beds, and, after awhile, disappeared in the shrubbery. When they were safely out of sight, he thought he might go out without fear of being seen, and hurried from the house.

Lena had asked him to come down and see Adrienne. She little thought how often, keeping himself unseen, he had looked upon the young girl's face, till it had become as familiar as his own shadow. He had clothed it in all the grace of fancy—in the idealism of a dream. True, they had never met face to face, but he had caught stolen glimpses of her rare loveliness. She seemed to him the concentration of all that was beautiful in nature and loveable in woman. He had watched and waited for hours to hear her footsteps as she passed—to listen to the rustle of her dress, or the melody she warbled, as she tripped along the solitary lanes or meadows between the Manor-house and the Rectory: He had been impassioned with the clear music that rolled from her lips; fascinated with delight, he would perhaps wander about the most lonely places in the neighbourhood, trying to keep her voice lingering in his ear. At such times the song of the birds, or the rustle of the stirring leaves, fretted him; even the music of the spheres, of which poets love to write, would have been unwelcome to him then. For awhile he could not bear to return to the rough sights and sounds of his old companions; they seemed to drag his soul down to earth, after it had been luxuriating in the heavenly music of Adrienne de Fontaine's voice.

"I am sure you will like her," Lena had said. Laurence smiled mentally as he heard the words. The idea of *liking* Adrienne!— why, she was a creature to be worshipped like an angel, not loved like a woman. He never sought an opportunity of speaking to her; it might have dissolved the mysterious charm that enshrouded her in his mind. Indeed, when, as in the present case, an opportunity occurred, he avoided it. He had a strong sense of his own unworthiness, and would not have presumed to address Adrienne in any other language than that of absolute idolatry. He could not have spoken to her as to an ordinary mortal. If anyone had accused him of being in love with her, he would have denied it. He was not so presumptuous as to be in love, after the fashion of man. He used his eyes to admire her; the labourers in the field might do the same. Hundreds, of high or low, might worship at the same shrine, which, in his mind, was sanctified to all. She was the one gleam of poetry that lighted his world of prose—his life of feverish follies.

Meanwhile, Adrienne de Fontaine went on her way, all unconscious of her sad, solitary worshipper.

CHAPTER II.

A WALK THROUGH LONDON STREETS.

"Thou knowest what a thing is Poverty
        Among the fallen on evil days;
    'Tis Crime, and Fear, and Infamy,
        And houseless Want in frozen ways,
    Wandering ungarmented, and Pain."

MR. CARLTON, anxious as he was to return to his own fireside, was compelled to remain in London two or three days. His business occupied him a longer time than he expected. He took up his abode, during his stay in town, with Mr. Creswick, a brother of Mrs. Carlton's, with whom he had been on terms of intimacy in former times. Many untoward circumstances had occurred to interrupt the course of their friendship, and keep them apart, until now. His marriage with Christina had united them again. They had parted, years back, in the flush of youth; the world, like a vast untrodden land, lay unexplored before them. Each had travelled a different way, gathering wisdom or gaining experience as he went. They had reached the top of the hill, and there met once more, when the autumn sun was shining on the earth, as on their lives. The harvest was over, the orchards were stripped of their rich fruits, the grapes were gathered from the vineyards, and the golden corn no longer glittered in the sunlight; but the rich fruitage of their lives was left to hang ripening in the sun of God's Providence, till His great harvest-time should come, and the fruits and flowers of their lives be gathered into the great store-house of Eternity. Their lives were fast falling into the "sere and yellow leaf;" but theirs was a hale and healthy autumn-tide, filled with robust and hardy strength, both morally and physically. Thus, in the autumn of their days, they renewed the bond that united them in their spring—the bond which was to hold them until the winter came, with its frost and snows, seizing with one cold hand the life here, and giving with the other the life eternal.

The characters of both gentlemen were alike in quality, though different in degree. They were both earnest workers in the field of humanity, but each laboured in a fashion of his own; they had both one object, one end in view, viz., the improvement of their fellow-creatures; but they slightly differed in their opinions as to the manner in which that improvement was to be brought about. Mr. Carlton made use, as it was natural he should, of such weapons as the Church sanctified, and placed in his hands.

These Mr. Creswick rejected entirely. While Mr. Carlton worked with careful caution and skill, fearful of offending prejudices unnecessarily, or rousing any antagonistic feelings in the class he wished to benefit, Mr. Creswick attacked them to their teeth, with arguments as powerful as a sledge-hammer; he tore their prejudices to tatters, and lashed, with biting satire, as keen and cutting as the north wind, the vices and follies of the day, sparing neither rich nor poor. He desired to show how much the misery and sorrow that exists could be avoided, and how often it is self-made. His strong healthy spirit would point out the cure.

Every man, he argued, must be morally his own physician. Sometimes he would send a bright stroke of wit flashing among his audience, till every face was lighted with a smile. Often he frightened his friends, and irritated his enmies, by the boldness of his authoritative language; provided he gained his object, he never cared whom he offended, or whom he pleased. He desired to make people think, and generally succeeded; he knew, if he could set the mind to work in the right direction, that thought would travel onward to the desired end, and reach the goal at last.

He had a great deal to bear in his stormy march through the world. The outworks which his moral philosophy threw up against the cannonade of his antagonists' pet theories, and ancient superstitions, were stormed and often carried by wise-acres and puritannic prejudices; but though they gained the victory, they bore signs of the struggle. Some sharp volley of satire, or barbed arrow of truth, shot from reason's stronghold, often battered the rusty armour of ages, and showed the weak places which time had already assaulted and corroded.

Mr. Creswick was never beaten. He issued from his citadel again and again, his wits sharpened at all points, and accompanied always by the sturdy giant Common-sense; it was astonishing what havoc they made between them. The enlightened few hovered for a time around the man who tried to circulate fresh, bright blood through the sluggish veins of the public, and then left them to prosecute his labour as he would. He was never daunted, but took the field manfully, and laboured from pure love of his kind, as few men labour, except for their own honour or glory. His name was held in high respect by many men of lofty rank; they appreciated his intentions, but disapproved of his mode of action. In our London Guilt-gardens, however, he was best known, best esteemed. He feared not to enter where rank vegetation flourishes in corrupt profusion, where vice and ribaldry ride rampant, the sole rulers of the soil; where squalor and misery issue from their fever-dens to inhale a fetid air, but one degree better than their polluted lairs; where haggard men, unsexed women, and emaciated children came forth and tried to smile when he appeared. They knew a ray of hope, a gleam of sympathy accompanied him, like a halo, wherever he went on his work of reform. He was their friend; the Dogberrys of the parish had no power to control his movements; the legislature no power to tie its red tape around his hands, till it became knotted in inextricable confusion. His hands were free to help them; his heart open to their sorrows. He came among them to teach, to cheer, and to relieve, for he was bountiful as well as rich. When gaunt starvation stared at him from hollow, hungry-eyed creatures, he first gave their body food before he ventured to feed their minds. A hungry man is in no mood for learning wisdom; Mr. Creswick had discovered that early in his career.

Few things gave Mr. Creswick more pleasure than to expound to his friends his theories, or to have a strong tussle in their defence with his enemies. The arrival of Mr. Carlton gave him sincere pleasure; he often yearned to renew his friendship, and his arguments, and propound his theories again. He was only troubled to find his old friend could make so short a stay; but he made the most of the few hours they were able to pass together. Many a pleasant story was told, many a cheering memory evoked, as they drew their chairs to the fire, when the day's business was over, and chatted in the old social way till the night was far gone. The past, the present, and the future—each was discussed in turn. They wandered from their own affairs, their own small joys, small cares and troubles, to the wide world, so prolific in the growth of human sorrow. Mr. Carlton was astounded at the tales he heard, from his philanthropic old friend, of the condition of the London poor; he fancied there must be some exaggerations in the pictures Mr. Creswick drew of the condition of thousands, as he knew, he said, that enormous sums of money were expended for their relief.

"And what is the use of money?" exclaimed Mr. Creswick; "that will do little towards stopping the rush of misery that is for ever sweeping through the streets of London. You might as well try to stop the flow of the Thames with a bank of rushes. No, we are the most liberal nation in the world, Carlton, but our liberality goes for nothing. We might empty our coffers into the cauldron of poverty, our charity would do no good, our gifts would sink to the bottom, and vice and want would still come bubbling to the top; we might give, give, the cry would still be 'give more!' All the rivers that flow into the sea will not still its everlasting rolling roar."

"Then must these terrible evils still go on?" replied Mr. Carlton, "if even you have no courage to attempt a cure?"

"Ay, but I have courage," answered Mr. Creswick. "I admit it is a disheartening, weary task; there is a moral ulcer eating into our social system, that must be plucked out by the roots. We know the cause of the disease, and it is our duty as Christian men to find a cure."

"I believe that ignorance, improvidence, and idleness are the three great causes of existing miseries, and they are most difficult to deal with," said Mr. Carlton.

"If we can cure the one, Ignorance, the others will do a good deal towards curing themselves. A wise man is seldom idle or unthrifty. Education is the remedy we must use for these evils."

"There seems to be a great deal doing in that way," said Mr. Carlton; "we hear constantly of the great efforts Government is making to educate and enlighten the poor."

"Bah!—child's play!" exclaimed Mr. Creswick. "Education is an exhaustless theme for a platform orator, who sees nothing beyond his nose—who, perhaps, spends his time in visiting charity schools, and training teachers to teach —what?—sol-fa, embroidery, the rule of three, and—I believe the rudiments of music was the last addition to the catalogue." He grunted, excited to a high state of displeasure. "A fine education, truly, for the labouring poor!— it does more harm than good. You might as

well attack the great toe to cure a brain disease. Besides, those who most need to learn
won't go to school."

"Then the teacher must go to them."

"In nine cases out of ten the teacher is as
ignorant as the scholar. He learns stereotyped
facts and phrases out of a book, and prattles
like a parrot by rote. If he were required to
explain the meaning of his own words, he
would be dumb. The teacher's book should be
human nature; he should draw his facts from
experience—his lessons from life. There's great
cry and little wool about this matter of education, Carlton; the subject is too slightly considered—too lightly dispatched. It is a small
thing among the great affairs of state; but I
fancy people forget that the small evil, if it is
not diminished, becomes greater, and may in
time overtop the greatest good. Ignorance," he
added, warming with his subject, "has before
now been the leader of a debauched and brutal
throng, that has surged up wave upon wave, a

very sea of corruption, sweeping through king-
doms, carrying away Church and State, burying
all in one common ruin. We must beware of
these things, and——"

"If the State so fails in its duty," said Mr.
Carlton, interrupting him, gravely, "try what
the Church can do."

"That would do little more, and little better
than the State," growled Mr. Creswick. "I
don't mean to depreciate you churchmen, Carlton; I admit there are many hard-working,
devoted men in the Church, who labour well
and with good effect. But there are not
enough. Too many of our London pulpits are
filled with pocket-handkerchief clergy, comic
actors, or brainless young gentlemen, who
drawl out dull platitudes to a weary congregation, whom decency cannot always keep
awake."

"No drawling tongue can spoil our prayers,"
exclaimed Mr. Carlton, perhaps slightly annoyed; " couched, as they are, in the grand,

sonorous, middle-age English, they have in themselves, to English hearts and ears, a charm that no tongue can mar—no time destroy."

"I was not speaking of the prayers, but of the after-course—the sermon," replied Mr. Creswick. "Unfortunately, men who have not the least notion of composition will write their own discourses; the consequence is, they dose their hungry congregation with half an hour's poor, pious, watery talk, that makes their hearers groan in utter weariness, and dread the weekly infliction."

"All men are not blessed with the gift of eloquence," said Mr. Carlton; "remember one half—nay, the best half of a clergyman's duty lies outside the church doors, in the homes of his people. Though he may not preach well, he may perhaps do something better."

"Very true," replied Mr. Creswick; "and if the clergy would unite together, and sally forth in one vast body to combat with the evil, it would succumb to their efforts. But they will not. They have not the courage to face the horrors which they know exist. As a rule, they will feed their lambs duly, but they will not go among the lean grisly wolves who prowl in the dingy dens and back slums of our civilized land. They extend their care to the rank and file Christians, who march to heaven under their banners, but take no note of those who wander from it. The forlorn hope in battle leads the van, but the forlorn hope of virtue is left struggling in the rear hopelessly, despairingly."

"The roll-call of God's host is sounded from one end of the land to the other," replied Mr. Carlton. "Those who refuse to rise up and follow must take the consequences of their folly. You would not surely blame a military leader for the disorderly conduct of his soldiers, nor a father for the faults of his family?"

"In faith, but I would," answered Mr. Creswick heartily; "for I should say the soldiers were ill-trained, the family ill-governed. The fact is, my dear fellow, you begin at the wrong end. You talk to them of heavenly things, and leave them ignorant of earthly matters. You talk to them of their future good, not of their present evil. You would point out to them the road to the other world, when their feet are almost hopelessly entangled in the labyrinthine terrors of this. Yet they must pass through the one before they can reach the other."

He paused a second, and then added earnestly,

"It is hard work, I know ; but we must clear away some of the difficulties, the pointed griefs, and thorny miseries that beset them *here*, before we talk to them of hereafter. A man with a starved frozen body is in no mood to listen to your lecture about the value of his soul. But come, finish your wine," he added, pushing the old ruby port towards his friend. "I am going out among my grisly flock; if you will ac-

E 2

company me, I will show you the sort of people
with whom we have to deal, and you will be
able to understand our difficulties better."

It was nearly eight o'clock in the evening
when they left Mr. Creswick's house in Harley
Street. They walked briskly, for they had a
long way to go. Mr. Creswick always took
those evening excursions on foot; he did not
like to drive in his carriage through those
wretched purlieus of London, that were filled
with squalid misery. He had a delicate feeling
that his affluence would contrast too strongly
with their poverty. He convoyed Mr. Carlton
through the narrow streets and byways of the
town, like one who knew every inch of the
ground he trod on. He wished his friend to
see the life of the London poor in all its
phases—the good and the evil blended together.
It was all new to Mr. Carlton, for at home,
at Crofton, poverty covered itself in decent
rags at least. Here it was naked, barefaced,
walking hand in hand with vice. They paused

once before a brilliantly-lighted gin-palace, that reared its brazen face among a nest of courts and alleys. From the wide open doors the lights flared out into the darkness, and the poor human moths fluttered in and out, till the last feeling of humanity was scorched up, and they were transformed to fiends. Women, blowsy and bloated with drink, tottered out with their emaciated offspring shivering in their arms. Men, unmanned, degraded, staggered about, with a dead despair darkening their hollow eyes, ready for evil, ignorant of good. Vice and want held their fearful orgies in noisy state; the very voices of the children were cracked and querulous. Here and there a poor pale face, that was evidently fighting a last battle against overwhelming odds of misery, glided among the reckless throng, and was swallowed up in the darkness of some dim alley, as in a grave.

"These are grim pictures of London society, Carlton, are they not?" said Mr. Creswick;

"these may be magnified and repeated a hundred times over in all parts of the town. What good could the most orthodox Christian do in this pandemonium of horrors?"

"It is indeed a very slough of despond," replied Mr. Carlton, "that might make even the Giant Greatheart despair. What can be done to help these poor creatures, who seem resolved to damn themselves?"

"Much, if we had the heart to do it," said Mr. Creswick. "You should see the places these poor wretches call 'home;' low-roofed, dismal dens, miserable cellars, where God's light can scarcely enter, and God's air is poisoned with the reeking filth that lies rotting on every side, where humanity huddles in such crowded masses, that every sense of decency or moral feeling must needs be stifled. It is lamentable, but scarcely strange, that they should turn ruefully from the horrors of home into the glittering temptation of these dens of Satan."

"It seems to me," replied Mr. Carlton, "that

the first step towards improvement, would be to raze these blazing palaces to the ground."

"That is impossible," replied Mr. Creswick, satirically; "this is a free country, where people have the right to destroy themselves, and disgrace the land they live in, as you see. The legislature has no power to prevent it. The one thing we can and ought to do is to give these poor ignorant people a clean decent home, and teach them the way to keep it. Let them feel the necessity of labour, and taste the sweet fruits of industry. Give them some healthy pleasures, to counterbalance the excitement they seek in drink."

They went on their way, and passed through other regions where poverty and decent labour tried hard to keep the wolf from the door, and live, but did not always succeed. There were old men and women, gaunt and thin, pinched with hunger, branded with sorrow, who had battled obstinately on the way of honesty, who had been tried and tempted, but never deserted it, but struggled on till their wits grew feeble, their hands helpless, and then crouched down in cellars or doorways to die. If Dante had lived in this century, and wandered through those scenes of horror whole districts in London present, he need not have wandered into hell for subjects for his "Inferno." He would have found them ripe and ready to his hand, bathed in the vivid light of a terrible truth.

Mr. Carlton gazed with wonder at the panorama of misery that lay spread around him on all sides. He would never have supposed that such things could be in a civilized land, and blushed to think that so foul a blot was allowed to rest on the shield of England.

"If these things were really known in high places," he said, "they would surely be looked to; it cannot be that they lack the will, but the knowledge to mend these matters. Ah! Creswick, if we could make photographs of all this degraded moral misery, and scatter them through our pleasant homes in town and country,

I believe every man, ay, and woman too, would rise up from their bright homes, and come forth to illuminate this darkness, yield up small pleasures to allay this great pain. I almost wish I had never seen these scenes," he added, with a sigh, "since I am so powerless to crush them."

"No man is powerless to do good in some shape or other," said Mr. Creswick. "Great things come from small beginnings. If every man would strive a little these matters would soon mend. But, come, we have arrived at our destination; you shall see how and where I cast my mite."

They turned down a narrow gateway, and entered a dingy sort of passage, which led them to a large square room, furnished with deal tables and benches; upon the former were pewter mugs, and trenchers with a good allowance of bread, the mugs filled with milk, a very innocent and wholesome diet; so thought the hungry hundred who surrounded the tables, looking with longing eyes, as they waited for

the word of command to move to the attack.
At one end of the board stood a mild amiable-
looking gentleman, whom Mr. Creswick introduced to Mr. Carlton as the Reverend Sir
George James Shuttlecock, "a good friend and
worker for a good cause."

Mr. Creswick's arrival—for he was the giver
of the simple feast—was the signal for a
general attack. Grace was said, and to own
the truth, but impatiently listened to; then the
wolves and lambs began to feed together.
Some among them were rough-looking men,
with louring brow, whom timid folk would not
care to meet in the dark. Others were poor
worn souls, who looked as though their whole
lives had been one long struggle with distress,
who had fought step by step singlehanded
against the giants—Want and Poverty—and
though sometimes sorely tempted to lay down
their arms, and take refuge in the ranks of
crime, had never faltered in their brave purpose "to die honest." God help them! Pa-

tient endurance is as heroic a virtue as bold adventure; though it makes no noise, and is not often recognized on earth, it will be recompensed in heaven.

When they had finished their bread and milk, they all went in a quiet orderly fashion into another room up the stairs, with whitewashed walls, and rows of benches, a raised platform at one end. As soon as they had arranged themselves, the Reverend gentleman took his place upon the platform, and commenced his discourse. He was an amiable, well-bred gentleman; he spoke well, with profound attention to the construction of his sentences, and the arrangement of his subjects. He chose for the first part of his discourse the delivery of the tablets on Mount Sinai; secondly, the beauty of the Ten Commandments, and the decree against those who broke even one. His polished phrases and rounded sentences fell harmlessly among his hearers; they could not understand him. His language was too elevated,

the sympathies too far away from the present;
they were heathens enough to find no interest
in Mount Sinai, and only associated the name
of Moses with the famous clothiers; of whose
gorgeous glories of plate glass, and wax figures
in magnificent and fashionable costumes, they
occasionally caught a passing glimpse. They
listened to him with respectful silence. A
stolid, stupid, weary look rested on the assembly during his somewhat monotonous discourse. They quite brightened up when it was
brought to a close.

"He is very mild, and does the best he can
for us," whispered Mr. Creswick to Mr. Carlton; "the poor people like him, though they
neither understand nor profit by a word he
says. Snobbery is confined to no class. These
poor, untaught beings dearly love the sound
of a title. However, Sir George is very useful; he presides at meetings, hands the prizes,
and sometimes gives very good advice to the
young people."

There was a general stir and sound of whispering voices when the reverend gentleman concluded; and Mr. Creswick took his place upon the platform. He did not lecture, he talked to the people, and encouraged them to ask him questions, or to answer those he put to them. He would sometimes give a shilling to those who answered intelligently, and to the purpose. He encouraged them to think. He spoke to them in their own homely fashion, used the simplest words, and the plainest imagery. He told pleasant anecdotes, that the most ignorant could understand. The history of a penny, told somewhat in Benjamin Franklin's simple, humorous style, created much amusement. The coin found itself creeping out of a poor man's pocket, at the door of a gin-palace. While ruefully lamenting its fate, it told its owner how much it had done for others, and how much it would do for him—how it would increase and grow, if it were put to its proper uses. The owner relented in his purpose, and the penny, after numerous adventures, nobly kept its promises. He introduced throughout the story so many humorous illustrations, that a rippling stream of laughter accompanied almost every word he uttered. It was evident that while listening to him, their friend and teacher, his audience forgot their trouble for awhile, poor souls! They were filled with new thoughts, new hopes, to carry to their dreary homes. Over all that swarthy, grim assembly, there played the light of intelligence, brightening their rugged features, and reaching to their souls. He never allowed himself to be interrupted; but when he had ended, he was glad to hear their observations. Mr. Carlton was deeply impressed with the sense and intelligence of some of their remarks. Mr. Creswick had the knack of extracting a spark from the dullest understanding. He knew how to make learning agreeable, and was in reality giving exquisite lessons of morality; while he seemed solely to amuse.

He tried to make them self-relying, self-respecting, and, above all, honest.

As Mr. Creswick finished, and sat down, the Reverend Sir George rose once more, saying,

"In his very eloquent discourse, my learned friend has forgotten one thing. He has omitted to impress you with the necessity of attending to those Christian duties which are necessary for your well-doing in this life, as well as in the life to come. I would advise all here to watch and pray, to attend regularly some place of religious worship, and to seek advice, in all time of trouble, of the spiritual directors of your several parishes."

He smiled benignantly, and sat down.

"I quite agree with all my honorable friend has said," replied Mr. Creswick; "but I must say I had not forgotten, for I never intended to remind you of your religious duties. I do not pretend to teach these matters; I feel my own incompetency too much to attempt to deal with such important affairs. There are many among you of different creeds—some perhaps of no creed at all. My lessons are for men of all denominations. I teach you your duty to yourselves and to your neighbours —I show you what you must do to become happy in yourselves, and useful to others. I leave to the clergy of your several Churches, each in his own fashion, to teach you your duty to God, and point the road to heaven. I show you the silver side of the shield. I leave it to your spiritual directors to show you the other, which may be golden."

Mr. Carlton was silent and thoughtful as they walked back to Harley Street. He was amazed at the scenes of poverty and vice he had passed through. How mild the diseases at Crofton seemed, compared with the fearful epidemic that appeared · for ever ravaging the moral life in London. He quite appreciated the sound, common-sense method Mr. Creswick took for the improvement of the people; though it must be confessed he would have been better pleased if a little more religious feeling had mingled with the course of instruction. He said as much to Mr. Creswick, who smiled, and shook his head, saying,

"No, I will have nothing to do with the religious part of the business. I confine myself solely to secular training and teaching. The rest I leave to the gentlemen of your cloth. This I must say, they seem to work very hard—but produce little effect."

Having transacted the business which brought him to London, Mr. Carlton was anxious to return to Crofton. In vain Mr. Creswick urged him to remain; he was gentle in his refusal, but steadfast in his resolution. "No," he would not be tempted—he must depart. Although he had been absent so short a time from the Rectory, yet it seemed to him like an age. Mr. Creswick was a most genial, kind, and attentive host, but Mr. Carlton's heart yearned for the bright smiles and pleasant voices that awaited him at home. He promised, however, that he would renew his visit to Harley Street in the spring, and render himself doubly welcome by bringing with him his wife and daughters. With this promise Mr. Creswick was obliged to be content. He accompanied Mr. Carlton to the railway-station, and there they parted, with many expressions and sincere feelings of regret.

Mr. Creswick waited on the platform, and watched till the train was out of sight; then he returned slowly and thoughtfully home, feeling more lonely and solitary than usual. The brief visit of his old familiar friend seemed to have given him back a portion of his youth. Now he was gone, and Mr. Creswick felt as though the brightness of bygone days would never come back so vividly again.

CHAPTER III.

A MIDNIGHT ADVENTURE.

" In fuller sight, more near and near,
The lately ambushed foes appear."

THE hours spent in a railway-carriage are generally among the most tedious and uneventful hours in life. Hills, valleys, trees, cities, broad winding rivers, even at times glimpses of the great sea itself, seem to fly past with such rapidity as to dazzle the eye and weary the brain. The loveliest scenery leaves no trace upon the memory; its picturesque beauty, shady nooks, and leafy bowers, so agreeable to the leisurely traveller, have no charm from the window of the railway-carriage. We may fly from one end of the land to the other, with no feeling save that of profound weariness, and gratitude when the journey is over.

It was seven o'clock when Mr. Carlton left London, and nearly eleven when he reached the small station at Crofton. No carriage had been sent to meet him, as he had not informed his family by what train he should return. He had depended on the village fly for his conveyance home. For some few moments he stood on the platform talking to the station-master, then bade him "good night," and passed out. The porter stood at the gate.

"Shall I carry your luggage up to the Rectory, sir?" he asked, touching his hat; "there's no fly here to-night."

"Thanks," said Mr. Carlton; "but I have no luggage except my carpet-bag—that I can carry in my hand. It's a fine night. I shall enjoy the walk home."

As he passed out of the gate, it was closed

and locked after him, for he had travelled by the last train. The station-master and porter had finished their labours for the night, and they went whistling on their way homeward, in an opposite direction to that Mr. Carlton was going. He had scarcely gone a dozen steps from the station, when he observed two or three rough-looking men lounging lazily by the hedge-side. He gave them the customary "good night" in passing, but they never answered him. From the momentary glimpse he caught of their faces, he felt convinced they did not belong to Crofton—he knew every man, woman, and child about the place. In one of them he fancied he recognised the messenger who had brought a letter for his son Laurence on the very day he had left home, and who, it will be remembered, had annoyed him by intruding on the lawn opposite the drawing-room window. He might be mistaken in the identity of the man, of whom, after all, he had caught but a momentary glimpse, but the fancy troubled him. The presence of strangers there, at that hour of the night, was suspicious, to say the least of it. Once, when he had got a few yards on, he looked behind him. They were whispering earnestly, and gesticulating, as though in some exciting debate. What could it mean?—what was their business there? They had not met there on that spot, and at that hour, he thought, for any good purpose, and if for an evil one, what was it? Whom did it concern?—whom threaten? Was it himself? and how, or why, should they meditate evil to him? "Pooh!" he scouted the thought, almost as soon as it presented itself; he would not encourage the idea. Why, might they not be honest labourers in search of employment? —homeless strangers on the tramp, who would take their rest for the night beneath the hedges? So he reasoned with himself, but still he would have been glad to find that he was once more safe within the Rectory walls. It was a long, lonely walk home—nearly three miles by the road, and scarcely a house by the way. Again he looked behind him—the men had left the spot where he had last seen them standing, and were now coming three abreast down the lane. Could they be following him? He quickened his steps, stretching his ears to listen as he went; by the sharp, quick tramp of their feet, he knew they accelerated theirs! For the next hundred yards, he kept the same pace, so did they, neither gaining upon him nor losing a single foot of ground.

"After all," he thought again, "their road may be in the same direction as my own; they may be honest men, whom my foolish imagination confounds with thieves and vagabonds. How my girls will laugh at me to-morrow, when I tell them of this adventure!"

In spite, however, of all his reasoning, he never slackened his speed, neither did they slacken theirs. He would soon know whether they were really trying to overtake him or not. There was a cut across some open meadow land, that shortened the distance to the Rectory full half a mile, and which was rarely used for any other purpose, as it led to no particular place. He resolved to turn into that path, and see if they followed him there. He reached the stile that separated the fields from the highway, vaulted over it, and started across the meadows without altering his pace. He listened anxiously to hear if the sound of their footsteps diminished in the least degree. No, they did not!—they came on with a quicker, sharper tread than before—reached the stile, sprang over it—they were on his track again! It was too evident now, there could be no doubt, that their purpose was to run him down—he had no time to consider the why or the wherefore; he must use all his energies, strain every nerve to outrun, to escape them. He no longer confined himself to a rapid walk, he ran, and ran, like one who felt his life hung on every step he took. They redoubled their speed, and followed now as though resolved to overtake him. Their monotonous tramp coming nearer and nearer sounded like thunder in his ear. Once he felt they were gaining upon him fast. His hearing, sharpened by danger, was so acute that he could hear their laboured breath hissing hot from their lips, as they speeded after him —human bloodhounds hunting their prey. Bent on evil, reckless, resolute, swift as they were, could he hope to outstrip them? Scarcely; already his strength seemed to be failing him; he felt that he ran with tottering, unequal strides; if he had paused, or in the least degree slackened in his speed, he knew he should have sunk helplessly to the ground. If the night had been dark and cloudy, he might have crept out of the way, and concealed himself in the long grass; but it was broad, bright moonlight—the wide, level plain he was now flying over, in such wild agony of spirit, was literally flooded with the refulgent rays. With what a cold, cruel, mocking light the moon shone down upon his flying figure, seeming to lend its brightest beams to guide his pursuers on his track. On they came, with the same rapid, unvarying tramp, and on flew Mr. Carlton, as though wings had been added to his feet. The profound stillness of nature seemed to aggravate the sound of the terrible tread of his pursuers. It seemed to swell louder and louder, to come nearer and nearer; to fill his ears, to deaden his senses, and lie with a heavy crushing weight upon his heart. His strength was failing fast. He felt he could not keep up this race for life much longer. He strained every nerve, but he fancied he should never reach the end of the meadows; the distance was interminable; in reality, they were scarcely a mile across, but the minutes seemed hours to him as he flew onward with incomprehensible speed. His pursuers ran till they were out of breath. They slackened their speed. He was struck by a sudden thought. If he could only reach the high road once more, he might hope to elude them.

Near the termination of the meadows. there was an old uninhabited house, which had been deserted for the last fifty years. It was in a ruinous, dilapidated state; if he could reach it, he thought he might perhaps conceal himself somewhere on the premises. It was his last, his only hope. Once more he gathered his energies together, strung up his nerves with the desperation of despair, and darted onwards. He came within sight of the deserted mansion. It stood about a hundred feet from the road, and had once been surrounded by a high brick wall, which was fast crumbling away, and was utterly broken down in many places. The house stood out, grim and dark in its dreary desolation. The window panes were shattered, the coping stones had tumbled to the ground, and the bright moonlight streamed in through the ragged roof, and sent its broad beams wandering through the lonely dwelling, illuminating the darkness with its ghostly gleams. Surely in one of those dim corners he might shroud himself in darkness and silence, until the hour of danger passed? One startling difficulty suddenly faced him. In order to reach the house he must cross the overgrown weedy space between it and the highway. It was impossible to do that without attracting attention, for it lay blank and bare in the moonlight, like a sheet of silver paper. His solitary figure flying across the green would surely attract notice, he would be seen to enter the house, and caught by his pursuers like a rat in a trap. His heart sickened. After struggling so far, it was hard to give way. The massive gates had broken away from their supports, but still hung obstinately on their rusty hinges. Quick as lightning a thought rushed on Mr. Carlton's brain. He had often passed by that spot in the day-time, and seen mechanically, without noticing it, a gap between the upright posts which had once united the gate to the brick wall, from which it had evidently broken away. The space was narrow, indeed scarcely a foot wide, but it might serve to conceal him in this his direst strait. Those who had not observed the gap in the daytime, could not have seen it now; for it lay in shadow, and seemed to be a continuation of the half ruined wall. He heard the ruffians gaining upon him, and with one brief, heartfelt prayer to God, he slipped into the aperture, and listened breathlessly to their rapidly approaching footsteps. Tramp, tramp, they came onwards, and paused within a few feet of him. He could see their swarthy faces louring in the moonlight.

"We lost sight on him hereabouts," exclaimed one, speaking in a low, hoarse voice, not much above a whisper, but still loud enough to reach Mr. Carlton's ear. "He must ha' gone into the old 'ouse."

"Not sich a fool as that, he'd know we'd ketch him there."

" He can't be there," said the other. "We should ha' seen him cross the green in the moonlight."

"No, we shouldn't," said he who had spoken first. "We kep' our eyes on the road, watchin' o' that."

" Who'd ha' thought the old bloke 'ud ha' gone skulkin' like this?"

"I never thought o' this cussed old tumble-down place, or I'd ha' kep' my weather eye open," growled another.

They wandered a little way along the road, keeping an uneasy watch on all sides—presently they returned, and slowly sauntered past his hiding-place. Again he heard their voices.

" He must be here somewheres; let's search the house."

" You two go inside," said he who had spoken first, and appeared to be the leader. " Where you can't search wi' your eyes, use your bludgeons; look alive, remember if he ain't there we're losing time. Sharp's the word. I'll wait here and watch."

The worthy trio separated. He who remained to keep watch strolled slowly up and down the road, glancing with keen fierce eyes on all sides of him. From time to time he passed within a few feet of the hiding-place of him they sought. Mr. Carlton's nervous system was so disordered by the desperate peril of his position, his senses so utterly shaken, that he could scarcely prevent himself from crying out. It seemed as though some horrible waking night-mare was pressing heavily on him. Those few moments were the most terrible of his life; the slightest movement, a sigh, even a breath, might draw the attention of his enemy, and cost him his life. He stood there in that narrow nook, still and motionless, his distended eyes fixed with a horrible fascination upon the ruffian who paced up and down so near him. Presently the searchers of the ruined house returned, unsuccessful.

"He's not there," growled one.

"You're sure?" said the watcher, eagerly.

"We looked everywheres. In the dark holes and corners, where we couldn't see, we flourished our bludgeons. If he'd bin there, he'd ha' cried out strong."

"I could take my oath it was hereabout we missed him."

"Perhaps the old fox is trying the doubling dodge. If he'd gone right on we must ha' seen him. I see how it is," added the fellow excitedly; "he must ha' leaped over the hedge and gone round Shallowell Corner. If he've done that, he'll turn up at the Cypresses. We'll catch him there, boys."

Off they started. Mr. Carlton listened to their receding footsteps with a beating heart. Fainter and fainter they sounded in the distance. He waited until they had died out, then, valise in hand, he stepped out from the narrow nook that had so effectually concealed him. He glanced along the road they had taken, and saw their diminishing figures far off; in a very few moments they would find out they were on the wrong scent—would no doubt return! Could he hope to elude their vigilance a second time?—scarcely. He was not far from the Rectory, not much above half a mile; but, unfortunately, nearly the whole of that time he would be in the full view of his ruffianly pursuers, as the road to the Rectory was on gradually-rising ground, and the moon still shone over all with its pale unclouded light. There was no time for reflections on the chance of life that was before him; every moment, every second was of consequence. With swift stealthy steps he crept noiselessly on his way, taking advantage of every bit of shadow chance afforded him. Once he paused to look back—they had discovered their mistake and were rapidly returning—another moment he heard their footsteps distinctly; they were gaining upon him fast. He had no strength now—he could not increase his speed. His limbs trembled under him, a sharp pain seemed to shoot up from his heart to his brain—a hissing, whistling sound filled his ears—he no longer saw even the moonlight clearly, for sparks of fire seemed shooting from his eyes. He came within sight of the Rectory. The family was still up—lights were glancing from the windows. They were evidently watching and waiting until the last train had come in, not knowing if he would return that evening or on the morrow. What a vision that first glimpse of home conjured up in the mind of the breathless, struggling man! Home it was, so near, and yet so far off! Should he ever reach it? He thought of his wife, his children, of the soft caresses and welcoming smiles that awaited him there—so near, so near, and yet so far off! A single cry would reach them, but he had no power to utter one; a gurgling, smothered sound escaped from his throat. He grappled with his hands as though he were grappling with something in the dark. He knew no more—everything was in a whirl of confusion—his brain reeled. The sharp peal of a bell rung out loud and clear in the night air, and startled the Rector's household. Mrs. Carlton, the girls, servants and all, rushed to the door, and found the Rector himself stretched senseless across the threshold of his home.

CHAPTER IV.

THE SPIDER AND THE FLY.

" Caught! caught! frail fool; in vain you fight or fly ;
You are your own dark mortal enemy.
Let flesh or spirit struggle as they may,
Law grips you fast, and Law will win the day."

MR. JABEZ JORLEY, of the firm of Pettie, Fogge, and Co., sat taking his solitary breakfast in the grimy parlour of the "Grapes Inn" at Crofton. He was evidently in an ill-humour, and disposed to quarrel with everything. He found fault with his tea, with his toast; one was cold, the other was oily, and the cream was no cream at all, but only a mixture of calves' brains with chalk and water. He cracked his egg with a sharp, spiteful tap, as

though he half expected to find a chicken in
it. He declared his sugar-basin swarmed with
flies, and a huge bluebottle was taking a pleasant
bath in his milk-jug; while the smaller fry, less
bold, contented themselves with creeping round
the edge, now and then dipping their tiny trunks
into the tempting flood, just as some human
flies creep and crawl upon the banks of life,
longing to taste its pleasures, but too timid to
face its perils. Between each sip of tea, Mr.
Jorley amused himself with worrying a bluebottle, which he had just rescued from drowning—he let it drag its long shiny legs half way
across the tea-tray, then he pushed it back, and
watched it begin its struggling journey over
again. Having amused himself as long as he
thought proper in that way, he began chopping
spitefully with his tea-spoon at the writhing
creature, till it was bruised to death; he then
flung it into his slop-basin with an impatient
"pish!" as though he was sorry the torturing
process was over. If there was one thing more

than another that Mr. Jorley loved, it was giving pain. His organ of malevolence, if there is such a bump in phrenology, was largely developed. He could not pass a worm without crushing it; nor see a moth fluttering round a candle without aiding its attempts at self-destruction. The human species he helped to torture and destroy in a different fashion: He sat there growling and grumbling over his breakfast, now and then muttering discontentedly to himself, as he glanced over a letter that lay by his plate. Occasionally he took it up, and read odd scraps of it aloud, making running comments as he proceeded.

"Humph!—suppose I am enjoying myself at Crofton! Oh! yes, nice enjoyment—got an obstinate pig to drive, that won't be driven, then get blamed for not bringing him to market." He read on a little farther, then added, satirically, "Squeeze him! what is the good of that?—get nothing more out of him, not even one's rights—I've done my duty pretty well, and squeezed him dry enough already."

Mr. Jorley seemed to cogitate within himself a few moments, then he pushed back his breakfast things, drew pens, ink, and paper towards him, and having hastily written a short note, rang the bell.

"Waiter, send Dawkes here."

In a few seconds the man who had startled Mrs. Carlton on the lawn of the Rectory made his appearance. He pulled his forelock on entering, and waited in respectful silence for the orders of his superior.

"Why were you not in the way last night?" said Mr. Jorley, casting a sharp glance at Dawkes's face. "I called for you three times."

"Sorry for that, sir," answered Dawkes, humbly; "thought I wouldn't be wanted arter the last job, so went to wisit a old pal t'other side o' Barnsy. Had to tramp all the way back, and got a little overtook, sir."

"Don't be overtaken again, my good fellow," said Jorley, with a peculiarly amiable smile, "or

you and I will have to close our accounts. It
would be rather a sharp reckoning, and the
balance largely on our side—eh, Dawkes?" he
added, with a glance of inquiry, that had something threatening in it.

"Well, yes, sir, I s'pose it would," replied
Dawkes, with a crafty twinkle in his eye, which
showed he did not consider himself entirely at
Mr. Jorley's mercy; "you allus take care o'
that, sir."

"Yes, always."

"But sometimes when a man's got a little
business of his own to look arter, he forgets the
balance on t'other side, sir."

"Sometimes," replied Mr. Jorley, emphatically ;
"but when such a time happens, it's likely to
be an unfortunate time for somebody, especially
when that somebody owes life and limb to
the exertions of those who shall be nameless.
But that's nothing to do with us, Mr. Dawkes,"
he added, cheerfully.

"Oh! no, sir, nothing at all," answered his

companion, who did not look quite so bold as before.

"What I want you to understand is this," continued his superior.

"Yes, sir," exclaimed Dawkes, anxiously.

"Those who are employed, in ever so humble a capacity, in the affairs of Pettie, Fogge, and Co., must have no other affairs, either of their own or other peoples', to attend to. You understand that, Dawkes?"

"Yes, sir, you makes it clear enough."

"The firm have comprehensive faculties. Where they can find one way to get a man out of danger, they can find fifty to put him back again. I fancy we understand one another," he added, significantly; "and now to business. I want you to take this letter up to the Rectory. Deliver it yourself into the hands of Mr. Laurence Carlton."

"I was forced to give t'other to the old 'un," exclaimed Dawkes, eagerly. "No harm come of it?"

"No, but this time harm may come of it. If Mr. Laurence Carlton is not in the way, wait and watch for him. Give this letter into no other hands."

Dawkes promised strict obedience, and departed. In a very short time, long before he could have reached the Rectory, Laurence himself sauntered into the room. He looked gloomy and disturbed. He answered briefly to Mr. Jorley's smiling salutation, then threw himself lazily into a chair, saying,

"Well, what news?"

"Not much," replied Mr. Jorley. "I suppose you've met Dawkes?"

"No, I've been down to the town."

"And he's just gone to the Rectory. You needn't be afraid," he added, hastily, as Laurence made an impatient movement, "I've given him instructions."

"To the devil with your instructions!" exclaimed Laurence, interrupting him angrily. "If you must send to the Rectory, I wish you would send a more respectable messenger."

"It would be impossible to find a more prudent one," said Mr. Jorley, soothingly.

"Pish!" exclaimed Laurence, as he turned impatiently to look out of the window.

"I see you are angry, but it is without cause. It is true the letter I have sent is of importance, but I have guarded against accidents. It cannot fall into your father's hands," said Jorley.

"It might as well fall into his hands as mine; better, perhaps, for the good it is likely to do," replied Laurence.

Mr. Jorley looked at him searchingly, not quite understanding his mood this morning. He wondered if he had made his father cognizant of his dealings with Messrs. Pettie, Fogge, and Co.; if so, how far had he trusted him? He asked no questions, but said quietly,

"That depends on which side you consider the matter."

"All sides are bad enough, so far as that goes," exclaimed Laurence.

"If you look at it from my point of view—" began Jorley.

Laurence laughed outright, but it was not a pleasant laugh, as he unceremoniously interrupted his companion, saying,

"Gad! Jorley, I have looked at things from your point of view for so long, that I can't see from any other.   But I must say you don't show me a very agreeable prospect.   From your point of view," he repeated, emphatically, "I can see nothing but my ruin and—your roguery. I don't mean your special roguery, Jorley, because you and I are very good friends—I speak of the *Firm* you so efficiently represent."

There was a slight touch of satire in his voice as he spoke.

"The Firm does not deserve abuse at *your* hands, at least, Mr. Carlton; it has always stood your friend."

"Well, I suppose it has," replied Laurence, reflectively, as though he had well considered the fact, and was loth to admit it.   "I dare-

say it befriended me in its own fashion. After
all, I don't want to quarrel with the firm—I
daresay I should have managed to ruin myself comfortably without any friendly assistance;
but you must own it lent me a helping hand,
Jorley. You can't deny that."

"You'll not have to complain of that
again," replied Mr. Jorley, quietly. "Their
hands are closing fast. Read that. I received
it this morning."

As he spoke he threw across to Laurence the
letter which had caused his murmurings a
few minutes before. He kept a steady eye
upon him, as he glanced from line to line.
When Laurence had finished, he threw the
letter on the table, tossed his hair from his
forehead, leaned back in his chair and uttered
the single exclamation—

"Well!"

"Well!" echoed Mr. Jorley, with a puzzled
expression of countenance; "I'm glad you think
it is well. For my part, I was afraid you'd

take it devilish ill. But, of course, I see how it is, you've succeeded in getting the money."

"Not a stiver."

"Perhaps the Rector has not yet returned?" said Mr. Jorley, inquiringly.

"Yes, he has," replied Laurence; "he came by the train last night, and met with a queer adventure going home; I have just been down to the police, to tell them to keep a sharp look-out on all stray wolves in the neighbourhood. But that's not to the point; you ask me if I have got the money, and I tell you flatly, no, nor am I likely to get it. I dare not ask my father for so large a sum—I have made up my mind to that."

"You should have made up your mind before!" exclaimed Jorley, angrily; "and not have played fast and loose with me, as you have done for the last three weeks. Why did you bring me down here——"

"I!" interrupted Laurence, opening his eyes;

"I never asked you to come. If I had been consulted, I should have advised you strongly to stay away. It would have saved me a great deal of annoyance, and you a great deal of inconvenience. I quite feel for Mrs. Jorley."

"Pooh!" he answered; "you must have known all along what the end would be. Why have you detained me here?"

"That's a question I have often asked my-self—I can't answer it, for, 'pon my life, I don't know. There's one thing to be said," he added, quickly, "I shall make no objection to your going back."

"That's fortunate," returned Jorley, drily, "for I return to-morrow." Laurence looked at him inquisitively, and with some surprise, but made neither comment nor remark. "You have read that letter, I suppose," continued Jorley, jerking his head towards it; "but I don't think you quite comprehend its bearings."

"I don't think I do," answered Laurence; "I am not a literary man, Jorley, you are;

and I must own there is a great deal there
that I don't understand; indeed, it's altogether
beyond my comprehension. Now, if you would
condescend to explain it to me, I should be
glad."

"It needs but little explanation," he answered
coolly; "if the five hundred pounds be not
forthcoming to-morrow morning by ten o'clock,
I shall be on my way to London at eleven.
At four the bill will be presented at your father's
banker's for payment, and the forgery of his
signature——"

"Forgery!" interrupted Laurence, starting from
his seat, with a white, enraged look; "you never
called it by such a name before!"

"However much I may have hitherto re-
spected your feelings, Mr. Carlton, I must call
things by their right names now," replied Mr.
Jorley, with a self-satisfied, complacent air. "It
is forgery—that is the right, the only word I
can use."

"*You* were the tempter!" exclaimed Laurence,

from between his clenched teeth; "in my worst and wildest fits I should not have thought of using my father's signature—the idea would never have entered into my mind, but for *your* advice."

"Pardon me for interrupting you, but if you will speak on unpleasant subjects, pray stick to facts. If I remember rightly, I merely suggested that such a thing might be done—I never advised you to do it."

"You knew I was like a drowning man, ready to clutch at a straw to save myself from sinking," said Laurence, in a voice full of con- centrated passion; "you drew the bill, placed it with pen, ink, and paper before me, whis- pered, like a devil as you are, that my name was worth nothing, but my father's would do all I wanted. If I signed the bill, you promised that it should never leave your hands until *I* myself redeemed it. I speak truth. You cannot deny that."

"I neither deny, nor admit anything," replied

Jorley; "you don't seem inclined to take up your bill, and we are not inclined to keep it. We can wait no longer."

"You *will* wait—not for my sake, but for your own," answered Laurence, with the calm tones of one who felt he had the game in his own hands.

Mr. Jorley leaned back in his chair, and looked at him with a careless, confident eye, as though he felt sure that, whatever card Laurence Carlton laid down, he held chief trump, and could win the odd trick. He did not speak. Presently Laurence continued emphatically,

"For that bill of £500, you gave me £120; and for more than twelve months I have paid interest at the rate of ten per cent upon the full amount of £500. You have still a rag of respectability to cover your legal limbs. If this infamous extortion were published to the world, you would be stripped even of that."

"Oh! we are very well able to take care of our own respectability," replied Jorley with a short cackling laugh; " fortunately we don't at all depend on the respectability of our clients. So far as *we* are concerned, you are welcome to make the whole affair public, at your earliest convenience. Of course we have a very great respect for you personally, but we must not allow our private feelings to interfere with our public duties; that is," he added, correcting himself, " with our duties as men of business. We regret that matters have gone so far, but the crisis has come. You yourself must see that, legally speaking, the right is on our side."

" Legally speaking!" exclaimed Laurence, passionately; but, restraining himself by a strong effort, he added with a forced calmness, " Well, yes, according to the letter of the law, I suppose you are in the right; but according to all moral feeling, you are as guilty as I am."

" Luckily for us, the law has no moral feelings," replied Mr. Jorley; " and you must be content to take it as you find it. I will try to arrange the matter in such a way as will make the payment easier to you."

"As easy as the devil makes the descent into hell," muttered Laurence; "go on."

"I will use my influence with Messrs. Pettie Fogge, and Co.," continued Jorley, "to induce them to receive one half the amount now, and the other—say six months hence?"

Laurence leaned thoughtfully back in his chair, and sat for some few moments buried in reflections. He thought of many things; of Jorley's present proposal among the rest. In the impulse of the moment he was disposed to accept it, for it offered him a reprieve from open disgrace, ruin to himself, dishonour to his name. Dishonour that might cling to his young sisters. The reflection of his sin might rest on them, cast a shadow on the brightness of their lives, blight all their hopes, mar their future prospects, destroy their happiness utterly. To visit the sins of the father upon the children is a divine prerogative only, and is performed

with divine wisdom; but man, in his shortsighted-
ness, usurps the right and inflicts punishment according to his finite knowledge. Thus it is that
when Justice has punished the guilty, and is satisfied, the world arrogates to itself the right to
pursue the innocent. Stealthy, noiseless, slow, but
sure, in every movement, it follows all who bear
the tainted name. Unseen, but felt, like a pesti-
lence in the air, it chills the warm current of life,
weakens the energies, and saddens the spirit—
makes gloom where there should be sunshine,
darkness where there should be light. Strong
men, who would face any known peril, dare any
visible danger, shrink away, and are bowed
down beneath that cruel cloud, which over-
shadows those who are akin to the sinner,
though in no way responsible for his sin. Laurence knew full well how much his one criminal
act, if publicly known, would injure his family
in the world's eyes, to say nothing of their
personal feelings of grief and shame. He could
not bear to think of it. He forgot Jorley's

presence, forgot his own peril, forgot everything, when he thought of his sisters, his father, and his home. He buried his face in his hands, and groaned aloud. The bare contemplation of the fatal act he had lightly committed, twelvemonths before, covered him now with terror. At that time he was associated with companions as wild and reckless as himself. They were all running the race of ruin, rioting in feverish follies and maddening excitements; it had seemed to him then rather a good idea to use his father's name; it was such an easy way of getting money. He had caught readily at Mr. Jorley's suggestion. Everything was prepared by that worthy individual, and made ready to his hand. He was tempted, and he fell. Thoughtless, unreflecting, regardless of the future, thinking only of his present need, he seized the pen, and signed his father's name. A worthless piece of paper in one moment became worth £500. He had committed forgery! As the pen fell from his hand, a cloud had fallen on his heart. It was light as gossamer at first; but it grew heavier and heavier, darker and darker, day by day. Now, in that one word "forgery," it burst and overwhelmed him. It had been written in spectral letters before his eyes, whispered in his heart, but never breathed aloud into his ear till now, when it fell from Mr. Jorley's lips. Laurence knew that his follies had wounded his father's spirit; now he felt as though his shame would break his heart; but the blow might be delayed for a time—Jorley had offered that. He placed, however, but little reliance on the honour of the firm Mr. Jorley represented. He had no faith in their forbearance or in their mercy, unless they were well paid for it; and he was helpless, penniless, a bankrupt even in hope. He knew they would exercise neither patience nor mercy for the mere purpose of saving a fellow-creature from ruin. After all, suppose they consented to wait one, two, three, even the six months, the end would be the same. He would live meanwhile a life of terrible uncertainty, with the sword of Damocles suspended above his head, which might fall at any moment and cut him off thenceforth and for ever from the social life of all upright honourable men. Worst dread of all, he would not fall alone; he would drag his innocent sisters, his high-souled father, all those he loved, down with him, and soil their pure name, spatter their bright lives with the mire of his sin. The thought, laden with the shadow of other thoughts, indefinable, but terrible in their indistinctness, drove him to distraction. He could not contain the agony he felt within his own soul; it gushed from his lips in a few wild words, unconsciously uttered, but uttered, almost sobbed, aloud—

"God help me! What can I do? What can I do?"

"Accept my offer, and trust to time and chance for all the rest," said Mr. Jorley, persuasively, in his ear.

Remorse and shame had almost extinguished the indignation that had flamed forth during the first part of their interview, when Mr. Jorley's words threatened exposure and disgrace; but now his voice, though soft, low, and conciliatory, had a startling effect on Laurence Carlton's spirit. He felt instinctively that the fair-seeming offer was in reality a ruse, to tempt him farther into the labyrinth of guilt, wherein he was well-nigh lost already. His heedless, indolent nature seemed to be suddenly awakened to a sense of danger. He felt as though he had hitherto been walking through the world as in a dream, with his eyes shut. They were open now, and he could see the perils he had passed through, and the still greater perils which lay before him. One step further, and he must sink into a slough of hopeless, endless evil. He felt that Jorley's soft voice was urging him to take that step. His eyes flashed fire, but he controlled his voice, and tried to speak calmly.

"No," he answered; "I will accept no offer —listen to no promise of yours. You are so confoundedly cunning, you cover the worst intentions with the fairest words. You speak to mislead, you act to betray. You want to hold me firmer in your power, that, when you choose, you may close your hand and crush me. No, let the worst come now! anything will be better —nothing can be worse, than the devilish uncertainty you have made me feel. You have held the threatened terrors of exposure and disgrace above my head too long. It has been like a continual nightmare, haunting me sleeping or waking. I can bear it no longer. Let the blow fall and crush me; I shall be stunned, and shall feel no more."

"Am I to understand, then, Mr. Carlton, that you refuse to take any steps——" began Mr. Jorley.

"I refuse to take any steps that may lead me nearer to the devil than I am now," said Laurence quickly; "I may make one struggle more to extricate myself, but I shall make it without your assistance."

"Good. That is to say, you will hang on your own hook," chuckled Jorley, struck by the idea that he had made a good joke.

"At any rate, I shall not hang on yours," said Laurence. "After all, I may manage to swing myself out of your reach with less damage to life, limb, or liberty than you may fancy."

He got up from his seat as though he meant to leave the room.

"Stay!" exclaimed Mr. Jorley, arresting his steps. "I have given you the best advice I could. You refuse to take it—and whatever happens, you have no right to complain. I have tried to be your friend."

"Oh! we won't argue that matter. I daresay you do your best, looking at things from your point of view," he added, with a short laugh; "*I* who have been so bad a friend to myself, have no right to complain if you have been worse. When a man throws his name, fame, and honour down in the mire, he has no right to complain if they are trampled down."

"You are trying to play the part of a victim!" exclaimed Jorley, "and, I must say, you do it very well. You have danced a merry jig to golden music; now that the time has come to pay the piper, you turn round and repay a just demand by unjust abuse. You pledged those valuables—'name, fame, and honour,' I think you called them, to us. Now we ask you to redeem them, you turn round and abuse us for having received them. We never sought *you*. You came to us all humility and smiles, wanting money, willing to agree to any terms to get it. Now you refuse to keep them! Bah! you are childish, Mr. Carlton."

"There's a good deal of truth in what you say," replied Laurence. "I admit it is cowardly to throw all the blame on you; but remember, I am like a man who is being stung to death. I feel a thousand pangs, and in my agony forget that I suffer from my own act—that I threw myself into the hornet's nest."

" And will not allow me to help you out of it," said Mr. Jorley.

" I have no faith in your good-will—I would not take it at any price!" exclaimed Laurence, with a touch of his old gay spirit; in a second it changed again, and he added with some emotion, " You are an old grey-headed man, Mr. Jorley; you saw me hurrying downward on the road to ruin—you might have stretched out your hand and saved me; instead of which, you cheered me on."

" I should as soon think of stopping a mad bull, as a young man in his ramping ride of dissipation. If he is deaf to the call of duty and the voice of home, is it likely he would listen to a musty old lawyer like me?" He paused a moment, and then added impatiently, " But all this bickering goes for nothing. It is a waste of time on both sides. I have told you what my instructions are."

"Well, I suppose you must carry them out," said Laurence. "But first let me understand my position perfectly. If I do not redeem my bill for £500 by ten o'clock to-morrow, you will leave Crofton, and by four in the afternoon you will lodge it in the hands of my father's bankers?"

"Your statement of the position of affairs is astonishingly correct," answered Jorley, amazed at the calmness with which he spoke of an affair of such vital importance.

"Very well," said Laurence, rising from his seat, and slowly crossing the room, "that's settled so far. You'll wait until ten to-morrow, to give me a last chance? Very well. The game's not quite played out, Jorley. Don't make *too* sure you'll win."

CHAPTER V.

MISCONSTRUCTION.

" To be wroth with one we love,
Doth work like madness in the brain.

. . . .

They parted ne'er to meet again,
But never either found another
To free the hollow heart from paining ;
They stood aloof, the scars remaining,
Like cliffs which had been rent asunder ;
A dreary sea now flows between."

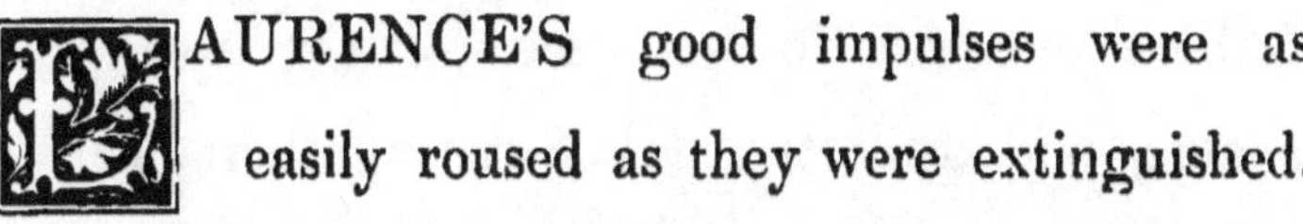

AURENCE'S good impulses were as easily roused as they were extinguished. Generous, warm-hearted, but weak, and unstable as sand, he had no power of self-government. His easy good-nature, his gay, genial manners, and vivacious powers of conversation, laid him open to many temptations, which a young man of a more phlegmatic temperament would have entirely escaped. His very virtues, loosely worn, made him a prey to the vices of others. His thoughtless good-humour became recklessness; his generosity degenerated into extravagance, and led him step by step into the Slough of Despond which surrounded him now. He looked about with his spirit's eyes to see how he could wade through it. He was so bowed down with shame, so burthened with a sense of guilt, that he felt as though he should sink at every step he took. There seemed to be but one way before him, and that led straight to his father's feet. Thither he must carry his freight of follies, open his heart, and let his father's eye look in, and see all the weakness, shame, and guilt that lay festering there, eating into his very life, tainting or destroying the root of all future good.

It cost him many a bitter pang to make this resolution; the best and wisest he had ever made. He took heart as he went along, roused his moral courage to the loftiest point, and vowed, over and over again, that nothing should make him alter his intended course. He arraigned himself mentally before his father's face, told the whole story of his life, from first to last, concealing no folly, omitting no sin. The thoughts, impulses, and feelings that had guided his wayward spirit through the years of youth to the present hour of degraded manhood, rose up in his heart, resolved themselves into words, and trembled on his tongue. He examined himself severely; he could look back and see where and how he had branched off from the line of right, till he had lost himself in the labyrinth of wrong. He could trace the cause now, as well as feel the effect, and was ashamed to see what petty stings had driven him so wildly astray. He would pour all his sorrows into his father's ear, show him all the inner bitterness that caused his outer acts, and bear without chafing any amount of reproaches his father might utter; he was broken-spirited, and knew he deserved them all. Many of the old tender feelings of his boyhood stole over him; tears welled slowly up into his eyes, but not one fell; with a half-sigh, half-sob, he drove them back. Man though he was, his heart yearned for the comfort of a mother's love. The memory of the old time came fresh and strong upon him. She had been his friend and confidante always; the soft reprover of his follies, the controller of his passions, the healer of all wounds, his consoler at all times. It seemed but yesterday that he had felt her last kiss upon his forehead, and heard her last words. How well he remembered them; they were lingering in his ear still. Almost unconsciously to himself he called on her name aloud; but she was in her grave, still and at rest; she could never console, never comfort him more. He hurried homeward, along the green lanes, as though he feared lest his resolution should leave him before he reached the Rectory. The trees waved pleasantly above his head, and the sun glittered on his pathway. But he felt no freshness in the breeze, he beheld no glory in the sunshine. With unfaltering steps he kept on his way. Again and again he repeated to himself those touching words of the poor prodigal, "I will arise and go unto my father, and will say unto him Father, I have sinned against Heaven and before thee, and am no more worthy to be called thy son!"

He had arrived within a short distance of the Rectory, which was only hidden from his view by a sharp curve in the road, when he was startled by the sudden appearance of the man Dawkes. It seemed as though he must have sprung out of the ground, for the road was perfectly clear a moment before. The fellow soon accounted for his unexpected appearance; pointing over his shoulder with a broad grin, he exclaimed,

"Bin havin' a quiet smoke in the 'edge there, while I was a-waitin' and a-watchin' for you. I wouldn't venture up to the 'ouse, 'cos I didn't want to be caught tresp'sin' on the Parson's grounds agin—he didn't seem to like it last time."

"There's a common road to the house, without trespassing; you might have taken that," said Laurence.

"I was to be extra pertikler about the letter this time," answered Dawkes, with a curious leer into Laurence's face; "I guess there's somethin' serious in it—a matter of life and death, one might think, to have heerd Mr. Jorley's diractions."

Laurence deigned to give no answer to these impertinent surmises, but simply held out his hand for the letter. Dawkes, in apparent confusion, fumbled in all his pockets, mumbling half to himself, half aloud,

"Sure, I can't ha' lost it."

"Lost it!" echoed Laurence, in breathless alarm, his face, more than his words, betraying the importance he attached to the safety of the letter. He had no time to do more than echo the words, "Lost it!" when Dawkes dived to the bottom of his breast pocket, and brought up the letter, saying, as he handed it to Laurence,

"There, there, don't be in a fluster—it's all right. You may be sure o' one thing, if I wasn't a safe card, Jorley wouldn't ha' trusted me wi' your consarns."

Laurence seized the letter, and would have hurried forward with a hasty "Good morning," but Mr. Dawkes wanted to do a little business on his own account, and was not disposed to part with him so readily. He laid his huge hand arrestingly on Laurence's shoulder. Laurence shook it roughly off, and indignantly inquired, "What more he had to say?"

"Not much," answered Dawkes; "jest a word of advice, that's all." He lowered his voice as he added, "I wouldn't 'ave anybody, as I wished well to, trust too much to Jorley. He's a dark hoss, and there's no knowin' which way he'll run."

"I don't understand your slang, nor what you mean by addressing it to me. If you have anything to say, speak plainly," replied Laurence.

"'Tain't allus easy to speak plainly," replied the fellow, doggedly, by no means pleased at the interruption; "'specially as I likes to put my feelers out afore I comes to the pint. Fact is, I know there's somethin' onpleasant a-goin' on 'tween you and *him*," pointing over his shoulder towards the village.

"If you mean Mr. Jorley, you are mistaken," replied Laurence, quietly; "he and I are very good friends."

"Gammon!" replied Dawkes, slyly; "young gen'lemen like you don't cultivate his acquaintance for the pleasure you gets out on it. *I* never mince matters, and the truth is, we're both in his power, more than either on us likes to be."

"Well!" exclaimed Laurence, breathlessly; from the fellow's face and manners he fancied he had by some means got acquainted with the terrible secret which lay between him and the lawyers. "Had Jorley betrayed him?" he wondered; surely not to such a fellow as this!

Dawkes seemed to enjoy the bewilderment that revealed itself in his countenance. He presumed upon it, and his manner was more confidential as he added,

"We can't neither on us do much apart; but if we was to jine together, we might 'elp one another, and shake ourselves free o' Jorley. What d'ye think o' that, now?—is it a bargain?"

"I should like first to know how far Mr. Jorley has trusted you with my concerns," replied Laurence, slowly.

"He trust! Lor' bless you, he'd trust nobody; he's as close as wax," said Dawkes, completely thrown off his guard. "He keeps everything dark—never lets no light into his affairs. But there, we needn't talk no more about *him*. We two will be a match for him anyways. I don't want you to decide in an 'urry; jest think on what I've said, and let me know what you're inclined to to-morrow."

Laurence felt relieved of a heavy load as Dawkes acknowledged himself ignorant of his affairs. When the fellow had at first attempted to talk confidentially to him, he had listened, and answered him, because he wished to ascertain to what extent Dawkes had become possessed of his story. It was quite plain now that he was only anxious to transfer his treacherous services from one master to another.

"I don't know what my inclination may be to-morrow," answered Laurence, "but at the present moment I am inclined to horsewhip you within an inch of your life."

He clenched his hand nervously as he spoke, as though he clutched a horsewhip and was about to use it.

"Well, sir, I'm sure I had no intention to hoffend. A friendly hoffer can't be no manner of 'arm, and if a bargain ain't struck, there's no hoffence on either side, I 'ope."

"Before you carry your next offer to market, make sure of your customer, rascal."

Dawkes muttered some apology for his mistake, and then turned rapidly down the road, leaving Laurence astonished at his sudden retreat.

As Laurence turned to pursue his road to the Rectory, he was startled to find himself face to face with his father. The Rector had lost his signet-ring during his terrible flight the night before, and, having made an unsuccessful search for it, was returning home through the meadows; he had, therefore, been a witness of the whole interview between his son and Jem Dawkes. As Laurence turned round and recognised him, he had just stepped over the stile into the highway. Mr. Carlton's eyes were fixed upon his son with a look of anguish, grief, and horror. He neither moved nor spoke, but kept his gaze on Laurence, as though he waited for an answer to his unspoken appeal. There was something in the expression of his pale face, white even to the lips, that froze Laurence's blood; for a moment he stood in mute surprise.

"My dear father!" he said at last, taking a step forward to his side, "what is the matter? Are you ill?"

"Ill!" echoed Mr. Carlton, and his lips contracted spasmodically as he spoke—"no, I am not ill;" he laid his hand on his son's arm as he added, "Who was that man?"

"What man?" inquired Laurence, amazed at his father's excited manner.

"He who has just left you."

"Oh! that's Jem Dawkes," answered Laurence, carelessly; "he has just brought me a message from a friend in the village, that's all."

"All!" repeated Mr. Carlton, and the cloud of anguish darkened and deepened in his eyes.

"All! yes," replied Laurence impatiently. "There's nothing very strange in my receiving a message from the village, surely?"

"No, there is nothing strange in that," said Mr. Carlton; "but to me it seems strange that my son should be conversing privately in the morning with the man who pursued me for my life last night."

Laurence looked in his father's flashing eye, and read there the terrible thought that had taken possession of his mind.

"Father!" he exclaimed; "can you suspect me!"

"Have I cause?" he answered.

Laurence looked round, and saw the figure of Jem Dawkes rapidly disappearing in the distance. In one moment he was after him, speeding like lightning down the road. He soon came up with him. In a second he had seized him by the collar, and was dragging him back to the spot where Mr. Carlton stood watching his movements in mute amazement. Neither Dawkes nor Laurence seemed to speak a word until they stood face to face with Mr. Carlton. Dawkes was a large-limbed, swarthy fellow, with a huge hand that looked as though it could fell an ox, or crush by a single blow the figure that held him so firmly in its grasp. They were a strong contrast, those two men. Dawkes looked like a giant beside Laurence Carlton. The one was large, heavy, and dark; the other fair, light, and agile, with nerves of iron, and sinews of steel. His long thin fingers clutched the sturdy villain with a firm strong grasp, as though he held him in an iron vice.

"Hold still!" hissed Laurence, from between his teeth; "if you attempt to stir, I will throttle you!" Turning to his father, he added, "Is this the man?"

He looked with a straightforward, honest look full in his father's face as he spoke. Mr. Carlton was so accustomed to his son's careless, reckless manner, that he was struck by the fierce spirit that animated him now. There was something dangerous in the expression of his face. His brows were knit, and his eyes darkened and gleamed with rage. His passions seemed in a moment to have risen to white heat. He never for a second relaxed his hold of Dawkes's throat. It seemed to want but the word of recognition from his father's lips to change that nervous clutch to the desperate death grasp.

Mr. Carlton looked from one to the other in mute amazement. He did not know the terrible position of his son's affairs, or he might better have understood the thoughts and fears that swept like a whirlwind over his soul. Again Laurence repeated the words—

"Is this the man, father? Look at him well, and answer me at once, yes, or no."

Although the Rector felt convinced in his own mind that Dawkes was one of the men who had pursued him—for he had not only heard his voice, but had seen him beneath the light of a full moon—yet he did not feel justified in asserting positively that he was guilty. He would not have sworn to his identity in a court of justice. He might have deceived himself, and in a hundred ways have been the dupe of his own senses. On his first appearance on the lawn of the Rectory, the man had made an unpleasant impression on his mind. In the moment of fright and terror, it was possible that the impression might have reproduced itself, and he might have imagined a resemblance where, in reality, none existed. No, he resolved he would not accuse, even to his own son, a man who might be innocent.

"I cannot tell," he answered, gazing steadily on the man's face; "now I look at him again, I should be sorry to swear to his identity. Let him go, Laurence; and rest assured that my would-be assailants will soon be discovered. The police are keeping a strict look-out. Do you hear, Laurence, let him go."

In obedience to his father's command, Laurence slowly relaxed his hold. Dawkes shook himself free, and darted down the lane; when he had got a few yards off, he turned round, scowled malignantly at Laurence, and shook his fist threateningly as he said,

"Mark me, young Squire, you shall pay for this in a way you least think on." He hurried onwards, and in a moment more was out of sight.

"I am sorry to have wronged you even in thought, Laurence," said the Rector, laying his hand upon his son's shoulder, with a tenderness of expression which he had not used for many a day; "but why will you associate with such a suspicious-looking fellow as that?".

"He is no associate of mine," replied Laurence, hastily; "he is merely a messenger from a friend in the village."

"Why should your friend need such a messenger?—the Rectory is not far off; he might pay you a visit there himself. In your father's house, Laurence, your *friends* should be always welcome."

"He is not exactly the kind of man I could

introduce to you or to my sisters," replied Laurence, candidly. After a moment's hesitation, as though he would approach cautiously the subject that was uppermost in his thoughts, he added, " one sometimes falls among thieves by the wayside of life, father, and——"

"And chooses to stay among them," said the Rector, interrupting him quickly; "but to such of your disreputable acquaintances you can hardly expect me to extend my welcome?"

"I don't ask it," replied Laurence, annoyed at the sudden change in his father's tone; "whatever my associates may have been, I I have never obtruded them on your notice."

"No; I give you credit for that," replied the Rector, his kindly tone returning. "You and I have been strangers too long, Laurence; we have been mutually misunderstood. We must understand one another better for the future."

"I trust in God we may," replied Laurence, fervently.

"I have sometimes thought that I have been to blame as well as you," said Mr. Carlton. "We will mutually confess our shortcomings," he added, smiling, "make up our accounts, strike the balance, and I hope go on smoothly for the future. But there must be no half-measures, my boy, you must give me your free and unreserved confidence."

"I will try," replied Laurence, mastering the emotion that made his voice tremulous. "I think I have got courage to speak out now."

"I will put you to the proof at once," said the Rector, stopping suddenly, and stretching out his hand. "Give me the letter I saw you receive just now."

"The letter?" repeated Laurence, completely taken aback by his father's unexpected demand.

"Yes, you cannot deny the fact that you have received one?" said his father.

"I will not attempt to deny it," replied Laurence; "but I cannot show it to you now;

presently, after I have spoken to you, or to-morrow, perhaps I may. Give me time to think."

"Give you time!" echoed the Rector, angrily, his old thoughts and suspicions—for which he had good cause—returning with redoubled force. "Give you time! Yes, that is, time to think how you can best deceive me. I see how it is, you would give me your false confidence, and abuse my true. By your pretended confession of past follies, you would gain the means to begin a fresh round of dissipation. I was mad even for a moment to suppose you could be honest."

The Rector spoke with strange and unjust bitterness. He had a minute before softened towards his thriftless son. He felt that he had wronged him by one suspicion, and like all generous minds, he was willing to believe he had wronged him in many. He was ready ·to open his heart and his arms to his erring son, if he would come to him repentant, like the prodigal of old; he yearned for a reconciliation, for their long estrangement grieved him secretly and sorely. But the reconciliation could only be the result of perfect confidence. At the first step towards a mutual understanding, his son had thrown a stumbling-block in his way. The first proof of confidence he demanded had been denied. He was irritated, and in no mood to listen patiently to his son's earnest asseveration.

"You wrong me, father. I swear upon my life and soul——"

"Your life!" repeated Mr. Carlton, scornfully. "What has your life been, but a shame to yourself, and a disgrace to me? As for your soul, when have you ever thought of that, except to swear by it?"

"Well, then, upon my honour, you are unjust to me now. I am bad enough, I know—I have caused you more grief and trouble than I ever can repay; but I am sincere now in my wish, in my intention to do better for the

future. I have resolved, but God knows," he
added, sighing wearily, for he remembered
how often he had resolved before, "God
knows if my resolution will stand."

The Rector answered with a bitter satire, the
remembrance of which smote him keenly in after-
years.

"You can support it, no doubt, with false
promises, false oaths, with anything but faithful fulfilment. No, sir, you have deceived me
too often, and I was fool enough to be almost
deceived again."

"But, father, if you would only hear me
patiently," exclaimed Laurence, still anxious to
clear himself in his father's eyes, but hesitat-
ing to do the only thing that would have served
his purpose.

He could not deliver the letter into his
father's hands. Though he did not know the
contents of it himself, yet he fancied it must
contain some allusions to the sin he was most
anxious to avow; but he felt it necessary to

prepare his father's ears to receive the confession. He would not have the sin he had committed flash upon his sight, painted by the coarse and vulgar hand of Mr. Jorley. It was bad enough to think the blow must be struck upon his father's heart at all. It should be dealt by himself only, and he would soften the effect by his real, earnest regrets for the past, and promises of amendment for the future. But the Rector was in no mood to hear him.

"Hear you patiently," he repeated; "you have exhausted my patience long ago; the time for hearing is past. This is the time for action, and the only thing I demand you deny me."

Laurence was about to speak again. He was heartsick and humbled. At any other time he would have answered the Rector with some sharp repartee or quaint extenuation. But now his brilliant sparkling spirit seemed quenched by the heavy cloud that rained down shame and sorrow on him.　He could only deprecate his father's anger, and plead for a patient hearing. As he attempted to speak, the Rector raised his hand with an irritable gesture, saying,

"I dare say you can be prolific of protestations, but they will avail you nothing now, for in future I must have deeds, not words.　I have learned before this how much faith is to be put in a reprobate's promises.　A few moments back I was almost willing to be cajoled again; but now—no," his anger rose higher as he spoke, "though you may bring to your aid hypocritical tears and whinings that would disgrace an upright man, they will have no effect on me."

Mr. Carlton's words had a marvellous effect upon his son.　The torrent of penitential tears and regrets that was ready to gush forth, bearing all his life's sins and follies before it, rolled back upon his heart, and lay there frozen, heavy, and cold, blocking up the passage of remorse.　All the old fiery nature revived in

Laurence's breast. The wild, wilful spirit that had been for a while dethroned, regained its place. His scheme for his own redemption was overthrown. He scattered his remorseful sorrow to the winds. His face was deadly pale as he answered his father's last words.

"No, there shall be no more protestations, no more tears. Through all my life you have mistaken—*now* you have rejected me. I hope—I pray to God you may never live to repent it!"

The reckless, despairing expression of Laurence's face was such as the fallen Adam might have worn when Paradise was lost, and he had no longer a hope to regain it. The tones of his voice smote Mr. Carlton's ears, and cut their way to his heart like a sword. Some sudden mysterious influence was at work within him, that quickened his pulse, shook every nerve, and stirred his soul with a sharp agonizing pain, a dread, a foreshadowing of—he knew not what. He could not have given his feelings words. His heart seemed to swell up into his throat, almost to choke him, and a mist was before his eyes. If he had obeyed his momentary impulse, he would have opened his arms, and, like the patriarch of old, "fallen upon his son's neck and wept;" but pride, that unseen phantom that stalks side by side with some of our holiest, purest impulses, threw its dark shadow over him. He drove back, he smothered the kindly spirit that was pulling at his heartstrings, striving vainly to draw him nearer to his son. He never spoke, he never moved, till it was too late. The expression of his face was frozen and cold—at least, so it seemed to his son's eyes. Laurence could not see the warm, wildly-beating heart that stirred beneath that marble mask. For some moments past they had heard the rattling of wheels rapidly approaching. Now, as they glanced up the lane, they saw Mr. Sterndale driving at a brisk trot from the direction of the Rectory. The last words had but just left Laurence's lips and stirred his father's heart, when Mr. Sterndale reined in his mare, and greeted them in his usual healthy, breezy way—

"Ah! Rector," he exclaimed, "I have been driving about the country like mad, and I do believe I have half-killed my mare. I was so anxious to be the first to bring you good news."

"Good news is always welcome," replied Mr. Carlton; "what is it?"

"Read and see," he answered, as he unfolded a copy of the *Times*, headed, "Defence of ——. Gallant Conduct of Captain Dundas." •

"You see what you will come to when you are seized with the red war fever," said Mr. Sterndale, turning to Laurence.

"Oh! if I take it, I shall die of it!" answered Laurence, with his old careless smile.

"God bless him!—God bless him!" exclaimed Mr. Carlton, as his eager eye scanned the brief record of his favourite's fame.

"You always said he would be a dashing, daring soldier; your words have proved true," exclaimed Mr. Sterndale.

"And he has no father to be proud of him —no father to hear his name made glorious by his son."

As these words broke from Mr. Carlton's lips, they seemed to be laden with all the bitter disappointment of his soul. They fell upon Laurence's ear, and made him recoil, as though he had received a blow. The gulf widened between them. He merely nodded to Mr. Sterndale, and would have hurried onward home to the Rectory, but the Doctor called him back.

"It's a long time since you and I have had a chat together," he said. "Come, jump up; I'm going a long round, all by Woodbury Vale. We can have a gossip by the way."

Laurence unhesitatingly accepted his invitation, and sprang into the gig.

"You can keep the paper, Carlton," said Mr.

Sterndale—" I dare say it will be acceptable at home."

Laurence raised his hat respectfully to his father. Mr. Sterndale smiled, bid him heartily " Good-bye," and drove off.

Mr. Carlton felt a dull heavy pain at his heart—an oppression as though a crushing weight had fallen on him. He stood still and watched till the sound of the wheels died away in the distance, and his son was lost to his sight. So they two were parted. If seas had rolled between them, they could not have been more effectually sundered.

CHAPTER VI.

AN ANXIOUS MOTHER.

" The rulers of the nation,
The poor ones at their gate,
With the same eager wonder
The same great news await.
The poor man's stay and comfort,
The rich man's joy and pride,
Upon the bleak Crimean shore
Are fighting side by side."

THE news of Captain Dundas's gallant conduct flew from mouth to mouth, and from house to house, until it spread from one end of the country to the other. Everyone seemed to have a vested interest in the young soldier. Before the day was over, the Rectory was besieged with visitors, eager to know more than Reuter's brief telegram expressed. They were, however, obliged to rest content with the scanty information contained therein, as no letters had been received at the Rectory since the last mail, and, of course, none could be expected until the arrival of the next. They never reflected that private and lengthy details of an engagement cannot flash with the speed of lightning along telegraphic wires. It seemed natural and right that Mr. Carlton should know more than the world outside, and they were disappointed when they found that he knew no more than themselves. It is astonish-ing how success, in any form or shape, elevates a man in the eyes of his friends and acquaintances, as well as in the estimation of the world in general. He may exercise the most heroic virtues, make laborious researches in the sciences, ennoble art and improve nature, yet die unnoticed and unknown; but if Fame takes its brazen trumpet, and sounds his name, it echoes from one end of the land to the other.

Men who have never noticed, or, perhaps, have long forgotten him, remember him now, and rise up, eager to claim his acquaintance. They rush back into the past, and gather up stray thoughts, stray words, small witticisms, wise sayings, or sayings that have no wisdom at all, things which have been uttered, and fallen unheeded to the ground, forgotten until now, that fortune smiles upon, and fame has crowned him. The sun that shines on a prosperous man gives glory and value to all that concerns him. His very follies are gilded over, and pass for virgin gold.

Long before the day was over, Mr. Carlton was wearied to death with curious inquiries. Rich and poor, from far and near, came trooping up the Rectory. Among the rest was old Kitty Davis, who seemed to be labouring under a slight sense of injury. She was one of the privileged poor who always found a welcome in the Rectory kitchen; however, she was not satisfied with the gossip of the servants' hall on this occasion. Since Captain Dundas's departure, she had established a kind of confidential intercourse with Lena, and often tormented that young lady with inquiries and suggestions respecting her son. She insisted on believing that he was under the especial protection and patronage of Captain Dundas, and ought to have a share in all his perils and in all his glories.

"She must see Miss Carlton," she said; "from her she should hear all the news."

Lena had carried her drawing, as she often did, into the most secluded part of the garden, where she could be alone with her own thoughts, and work or dream, at her own pleasure. Old Kitty, however, soon found her way to Lena's cosy nook, and disturbed the course of her pleasant thoughts.

"I know'd you'd forgive me intrudin', Miss Lena, but I want to know all abouten everything, and I know'd you could tell me."

"What! about everything? Why, how wise you must think me!"

"Ah! Miss Lena," replied the poor soul, shaking her head; "you know 'everything' means my Joe, for he is everything to me. I want to know something abouten him; for there isn't a braver nor a better lad gone to the war nor he is."

Lena's knowledge of Joe was limited. She remembered him only as a red-headed mischievous urchin who was employed by the neighbouring farmers as scarecrow general to frighten the birds. However, she sympathised with the widow's admiration for her only son, and answered her with a smile, saying that "she was sure he was a good lad, and would be a credit to his mother."

"Ah! he'll be a credit to his country too, Miss Lena; he'd run his head agin a stone wall, or load a gun wi' his own limbs, and be fired off on the Rooshuns, if he thought it 'ud be any good to his country. But just tell me what the paper says abouten him—if it won't give you too much trouble, Miss."

"Really," answered Lena kindly, "there is nothing in the paper that will interest you; it merely says that a great battle has been fought and we have won—nothing more."

"But it says somethin' about the Captain, doesn't it?"

"Oh! yes," replied Lena, as her pulse quickened and a proud blush suffused her cheeks; "but it only says that he did his duty bravely, as of course he would."

"And so would my Joe," rejoined the widow stoutly. "You're sure they don't mention him, Miss? for wherever the Captain was, he was too."

"That could hardly be," replied Lena, half laughing, yet getting almost angry at hearing Joe's name coupled with that of Archibald Dundas. "Remember your son is in quite a different regiment; besides, the private soldiers who follow their officers in a mass, have not the same chance of distinguishing themselves as those who lead them."

"It don't matter about that," answered Kitty. "If it hadn't abeen for the Captain, my Joe 'ud never ha' thought o' sodgerin'— and wherever the Captain goes, I know my boy 'll stick to him."

Lena knew it would be useless to argue with the old woman, or attempt to suggest the improbability of their ever meeting, or of Archie's recognizing her son even if they did. The poor soul obstinately constituted Captain Dundas as her Joe's guardian, and would not have her belief disturbed. It was a comfort to her to fancy there was a friend watching over him in that far-off land. The kind of self-deception in which she indulged did no harm to anyone, and was a great comfort to herself, so Lena said nothing to shake her faith. She assured Kitty that whenever any details of this, or any other battle or skirmish, arrived, she would communicate all the news to her.

"God bless you, Miss Lena, if you'd only tell

me everything yourself! Other folks laugh at me when I talk of my boy, and I dare say I talk too much. I forget he's nothing to them, though he's all the world to me. I'm so lonesome without him. He's never out o' my thoughts, Miss Lena. I keeps his place allus ready for him, and I trail up the bits o' flowers he was so fond on. My memory isn't so good as it was, Miss, for whiles I forget he's left me, and hark to hear him whistlin' as he comes home from his work; then I remember he's gone where his mother's love can't foller him—perhaps I'll never see him agin any more."

"But indeed I hope you will," replied Lena cheerily. "Come, you mustn't be downhearted. Only fancy, when the war is over, he may come back in triumph, how proud you will be! And perhaps the whole village will turn out with drums and fifes to meet him!"

"And I'd hear them, Miss Lena," replied the old woman, brightening up and clasping her withered hands—"I'd hear them though I'm sleeping in my grave! Does the Captain ever speak on him in his letters?" she added, looking eagerly into Lena's face. "I know I'm makin' free to ask—but if I could only see his name wrote down, though I couldn't read it—it 'ud be a comfort to me." Lena smiled to herself at the idea of Archibald making Joe the subject of his letters; but she answered readily,

"Well, no, Kitty, he never speaks of him; you know he has so much to think of and to write about. However, the next time we write to Captain Dundas, we will make special inquiries about your son."

"Will you indeed?" exclaimed Kitty gratefully. "Ah! you've got a kind heart, Miss Lena, and it isn't the thanks of such as me that'll ever repay you. But when the last hour comes (and I hope it'll be long before it comes to you), for we must all die, high and low, rich and poor, it isn't the thoughts of your beauty or your pleasure that'll give you comfort then. It's the good you've done, and the friend you've been to the poor and lonely like me, that'll be a blessin' to you then, when this world can do nothin' more to ease you."

Lena was touched by the poor widow's feeling tones and simple eloquence.

"If you talk like that," she said, "you will make me ashamed of having done so little."

"I hope you'll live to do plenty more, Miss Lena; and if I get to heaven first, I'll pray for you, and the prayers of a poor old crittur like me can't do you no harm—no harm," repeated Kitty; and after a moment's pause, following the thought that lay nearest to her heart, she added, "But you'll be sure to ask about my Joe—you'll try not to forget, Miss Lena?"

Lena promised, again and again, to endeavour to gain some reliable information concerning him. She kept her word. For some time longer she listened patiently to the poor mother's garrulous regrets, mingled with curious details of her domestic troubles, and sympathised with and consoled her, endeavouring to excite her pride, and build her hopes upon her son. After awhile Kitty departed, and carried away a lighter heart than she had brought with her.

Lena, once more left alone with her own thoughts, tried to gather up the broken links that had been so unceremoniously snapped asunder. She was loath to return to the house. The luncheon bell rang, but she could not bring herself to rejoin the family. It was so delightful to be alone, with nothing to do, nothing to distract her attention from the thoughts of him.

She lingered long in the bright sunshine, playing with her graceful thoughts, listening to the mysterious murmuring of fancy, which has always some pleasant tales to whisper in the ears of youth. What a joyous time it is! that spring-tide of early years, when life, in all its vigorous freshness, leaps through the veins, making the pulse beat and the spirit glow with the glory of living, seeking nothing, caring for nothing, beyond the enjoyment of the present hour; satisfied with the mere fact of being here, in this teeming world of beauty, with power to hear, to see, to feel the wondrous greatness of nature, so harmonious and exhilarating in all her works. What unconscious joy we gather from the perfume of a flower, the soft soughing of the breeze, or the rippling murmur of a stream! As years pass on, the romance of the heart begins, some sweet and softly flowing on, ending in peace; others more turbulent, and full of broken lights and shadows. Wild untrained hopes stretch luxuriantly on every side, clinging to whatever offers to support them, and the thoughts and feelings, tremulous and passion-stained, go wandering up and down through the soul's sanctuary; as we see in our dreams, the grey shadows, wandering through the dim aisles of some cathedral, while the mysterious light from the outer world glides down upon them through the antique windows of stained glass, and pouring a broken mass of colour, now bright, now dim, upon those who wandered up and down, resting never until they reach the grave. Every heart has its own romance, of which, perhaps, the world knows nothing. Some are uttered aloud, and cry out for sympathy; others written on the face in thin lines of passion, full of emotion, now thrilling with enthusiasm, then poignant with regrets, at last washed out in tears of blood. Some there are that are never written at all, but reveal themselves in actions; with them romance becomes reality, and goes out into the world, clothed in its own truth and purity, though the blind old world sees nothing but the plain prosy form of sober every-day life. It hears nothing of the undercurrent of poetry that makes the heart thrill to music of its own making.

In some natures the spirit of romance exhausts itself quickly. It is like a brief dream, soon over; the glow fades from it, and as years roll on, and bear it away farther and farther into the past, we look back upon it with mournful eyes, for we know that it is dead and buried with the days of our youth, that can never, never return again. We dash away the blinding tear, turn from the past to the future. A sovereign voice, throned in our own souls, commands us to take up our burthen and march onwards, to waste no time in vain regrets, but go forward and enjoy the good that remains to us. For though friends and fortune change, and our hopes still deceive, delude us, nature is always true to us, ready at all times to delight, to instruct, and to console us—to teach us some bright lesson of faith, of patience, and endurance. It is as though the divine voice was still lingering among the fruits and flowers of earth, speaking to the heart as audibly as thunder speaks to the ear. Is it not Drexilius who represents the rose, addressing the beholder, saying, "See how against the injuries of night I close my contracted globe, and again unfold its beauty at the rising sun—mark how admirable is the order, colour, form, and odour of my leaves; and when you admire me, refer your love and wonder to my Maker." After all, in spite of carking cares, delusive hopes, and dull realities, it is a glorious thing to live, to walk through this beautiful world, to be in it and of it, the most grand and glorious creatures God has made.

Lena lingered long in "her bower of roses," nursing her soul's romance, making her thoughts ladders, on which her love might climb to heaven. She knew that when she returned to the house, she should hear his name on every lip— they all would unite to eulogise and praise him. She would rather have remained there, alone with her own thoughts; she was ashamed to show even to those who were nearest and dearest to her, how proud and happy she was; she knew that they could read it in her face. Presently the skies clouded slowly over, and big rain-drops began to fall. Then she remembered the words of the poet who says that "rain-drops are the tears that angels shed for the sorrows of humanity." Her thoughts flew off to that distant battle-field; she wondered if rain was falling there? washing the wounds and bathing the parched lips of the bleeding and the dying.

As she hurried across the lawn towards the house, she saw Laurence coming along the opposite path. She waited, in order to give him time to reach her, that they might walk on together. As he came nearer, she fancied he did not see her. She called to him; he never answered, but branched off into a narrow pathway which led to the kitchen-garden, through that to the back of the house. It was evident now that he purposely wished to avoid her. From the momentary glimpse she caught of his face, she saw there was an expression of dark settled gloom upon it, which terrified her. She lost no time in thinking or wondering, but hurried along, entered the house, and reached the back entrance just as he crossed the threshold. She caught him by the arm, exclaiming,

"Why, Laurence, what has happened? You look as though you had been undergoing some awful trial!"

"So I have," he answered grimly; "I have been struggling with a deadly enemy—and worst of all, Lena, my enemy has won."

CHAPTER VII.

DEEPER AND DEEPER STILL.

" The wild prospect when the soul reviews,
All rushing through their thousand avenues,
The hopeless past, the hasting future, driven
Too quickly on to guess of hell or heaven ;
Deeds, thoughts, and words, perhaps remembered not
So keenly till that hour, but ne'er forgot ;
Things light or lovely in their acted time,
But now to stern reflection each a crime ;
The withering sense of evil unreveal'd,
Not cankering less because the more concealed."

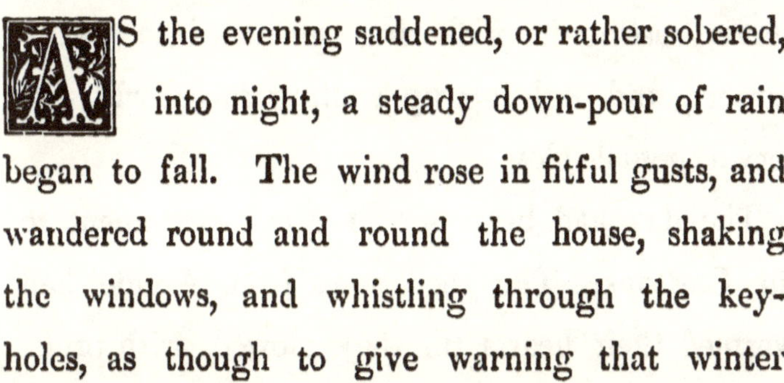

AS the evening saddened, or rather sobered, into night, a steady down-pour of rain began to fall. The wind rose in fitful gusts, and wandered round and round the house, shaking the windows, and whistling through the key-holes, as though to give warning that winter was slowly travelling from the far north, and would soon stand shivering at the gate in his robe of fallen snow.

Although it was still only autumn, the evenings had become damp and chilly, and brought with them a conviction that summer had indeed departed. There is, perhaps, nothing more gloomy and depressing than those grey-tinted hours that hover between the closing of the bright, and opening of the dreary, season of the year. It is neither one thing nor the other; neither all fair, nor all the reverse. Everyone is discontented, and more or less affected by it. The smart ornament is taken out of the grate, and a blazing fire takes its place, sending out a pleasant fragrance into the humid atmosphere, casting its flickering gleams into dusky corners, and lighting up smiling faces with its fervid genial glow.

The day had been one of great excitement to the Carltons. The good news from Archie had warmed their hearts till they glowed, with pride, hope, and love for the absent one. They were all, with the exception of Laurence, assembled round a blazing fire in the drawing-room. The curtains were drawn, and the light of the fire threw a blood-warm tint upon them all as they sat chatting over the events of the day. A pleasant babbling stream of conversation flowed from lip to lip; memory of the past blended with the glory of the present, and ambitious hopes for the future of Captain Dundas. More than once Mr. Carlton led the conversation into a different channel, but it always drifted back to Archie. Presently the Rector's face clouded over—he became absent and thoughtful; perhaps the contrast between Archibald and Laurence struck him at that time with painful force. The one was reaping the field of honour and glory, winning golden opinions of all sorts of men, and doing his duty manfully in the path of life he had chosen. The other was reaping as he had sown, in a field of bitterness and sorrow. The wine of life had been spilt before it had reached his lips. He had gone into the world with a prospect fair and promising. An honourable and profitable career had been open to him; but he had turned aside, and brought home nothing, save shame for the present, despair for the future. Some such reflections as these evidently filled Mr. Carlton's mind. When Lena brought the chess-board, for him to play his customary game before retiring to rest, he declined, saying,

"I don't feel inclined to exert my brain to-night, Lena. Where's Laurence? He must take my place. I know you hate to be beaten, and you'll find him an easy conquest."

"I don't think he is at home," said Mrs. Carlton. "I have not seen him since the morning."

"I have," said the Rector, drily.

"So have I," exclaimed Lena. "He came in with me just as the rain began, and I don't believe he has gone out since."

"Fetch him," said Mr. Carlton.

Lena gladly went on her errand. It was seldom the Rector inquired for his son, and his doing so now seemed to betide well for Laurence. So thought Lena, as she tripped lightly up the stairs, and tapped at her brother's door.

" Laurie !"

" Who's there ?"

" I—Lena."

" Well ?"

" Papa wants you in the drawing-room."

" What for ?"

" To play a game of chess with me."

" Pshaw !" exclaimed Laurence. " Tell him I am busy writing letters, and can't come."

" Open the door, I want to come in." As she spoke, Lena gave the handle of the door a gentle rattle. He admitted her at once. " I must teach you good manners, Master Laurie," she said, as she stepped inside. " Don't you know that it is very rude to speak to a lady through closed doors ?"

" I will take you for my model, and mend

my manners," he said, smiling; "but as a rule I do not admit curiosity within my sanctum."

"You said you were writing letters," said Lena, glancing sharply round the room, "and yet there's no sign of pen, ink, or paper anywhere."

"Pens, ink, and paper are mere vulgar accessories, Lena; quite secondary considerations in my case. I write my letters in my head first, and sometimes don't put them on paper for a month afterwards. At this moment I am busy concocting a letter which I intend to write home from America, as soon as I have been there and made my fortune."

"What nonsense!—do come downstairs. Papa will wonder why I am staying so long."

"I cannot—I have told you I am busy."

"Papa seems to wish it to-night. I don't think he's very well; his nerves were so shaken last night, he has not recovered himself yet."

"What does he say?" exclaimed Laurence,

eagerly. "Has he been dwelling on that subject again?"

"No," replied Lena, "he does not speak of it at all; on the contrary, I fancy he seems to shun the subject. What do you mean?"

"Nothing, Lena," he answered, after a moment's pause; adding, with great excitement, "my father knows I am a thriftless fool, and he suspects me to be a villain as well."

"Oh! Laurie, brother, I wish you and papa could understand one another better."

"We never shall in this world," he answered. "There, go downstairs, Lena, it is no use looking so wistfully at me; I am not fit company for a cheerful family to-night—I should act as a general wet blanket, and throw a damp over the whole of you. Give me a kiss, and go. I have said nothing to vex you, have I?"

Lena twined her arm fondly round him, and made a last effort to coax him to join them, but in vain. She was compelled to go back to the drawing-room without him. She accounted for his non-appearance, saying,

"He says he is very busy writing letters, papa."

"His correspondence seems to be increasing," said the Rector, with a sigh of disbelief. "Put away the chess-board, Grace, and play something."

"You must consent to be spoilt and petted as an invalid for to-night," said Mrs. Carlton; "come, sir, throw aside 'Blackstone,' take possession of the sofa, and be amused for the rest of the evening. You really do look ill."

"I am not quite so young as I was. There, that will do," he added, smiling gratefully in her face, as she arranged and re-arranged the cushions with scrupulous care; "if you treat me like this, I shall be tempted to become an invalid in earnest, for the mere pleasure of being so agreeably spoilt. You need not put away the chess-board, Gracey; you girls can play your game, and, Christina, you sing to me."

" You are a privileged tyrant for to-night," said Mrs. Carlton, as she began turning over a packet of new music that had just arrived from London. " What will you have?"

" Oh! none of those will suit my present mood," he answered; "sing some of the familiar music of old times—it reminds one so pleasantly of the days that are gone."

" I should think that was anything but a pleasant reminder," exclaimed Grace; "for my part, if there is a thing I mortally detest, it is thinking of a pleasure that is gone, and feeling it can never come back again."

" You are not old enough yet to appreciate the pleasures of memory," replied her father.

" I prefer the pleasures of hope," said Grace.

" Well, at your age, perhaps hope is the most natural and agreeable acquaintance. As you grow older, you will find that memory is your best friend; in her sweet companionship you may live over again some of the happiest hours of your life."

Mrs. Carlton had meanwhile seated herself at the piano, and her hands wandered for a moment restlessly over the keys, as though she was searching for some hidden melody, that would not rise at her bidding. She found it at last, and as she struck the first few notes, the Rector recognised the prelude to that most perfect gem of a great master, " What, though I trace each herb and flower."

"Glorious, grand old Handel!" he exclaimed; "you could have chosen nothing I love better." Mrs. Carlton's sweet voice rose with its rich, rare burthen of melody, and poured forth the solemn strain of the music-poet with exquisite purity and feeling. The spirit of the dead composer might have inspired her with something of his own feeling, so touchingly she embodied the soul of his genius; a serene holy calm seemed to fall upon her hearers, as they listened with breathless attention to her up-soaring tones. The girls neglected or forgot their game. The Rector lay back on the sofa with closed eyes, scarcely seeming to breathe, listening with rapt, reverential awe to those entrancing sounds which are so well calculated to carry the soul up to the throne of that immortal God in whose honour they were created.

While they were enjoying these refined pleasures in the drawing-room, Laurence sat in his solitary chamber above, listening, with an aching heart, to the swelling sounds that stole with occasional distinctness to his ear. He pictured the family group—his father nobly grand and serene, resting after his day's labour; his blooming sisters, with smiling, happy faces, lending cheerfulness as well as beauty to the domestic scene; and Mrs. Carlton, in her glorious maturity, presiding over all the genius of home. As he saw them, in his mind's eye, assembled in sweet peace and concord, he half wished he had gone down with Lena, to make one, perhaps for the last time, of the family picture. He was half inclined to creep downstairs, and join them even now; he felt it would do his sick spirit good to breathe that pure atmosphere of melody and peace; but the dread of meeting his father's face withheld him. The busy hum of voices arose when the music ceased. After a while he heard the bell ring, and he knew the household was gathered together for family prayer; then all was still, except the Rector's deep sonorous voice, as he read the simple, but impressive service he had chosen. Laurence heard almost every word, and the deep monotone of his father's voice, as he prayed earnestly for all "who were in sorrow or distress," affected him deeply; he buried his face in his hands, and though his lips never moved, his heart joined fervently in supplication to God.

Presently he heard the opening and shutting of doors, kind "good nights" exchanged, light-falling feet, and soft girlish laughter on the stairs. He knew the family had separated, and were all retiring to rest. When all was still, and profound silence reigned throughout the house, he felt as though he were doubly an outcast—doubly forlorn. For a long time he sat there, gazing moodily upon the dying embers that were still smouldering in the grate. He never thought of following the example of the rest of the household by retiring to rest, for he knew he could not sleep. A crisis in his life was coming—must come with the fast-approaching morrow. What would that crisis be?—how would that morrow end? Whatever happened, he knew must bring shame and disgrace to him, but not to him only. Could all the accumulated evil he dreaded fall on his head alone, he would have borne it bravely, without a murmur, without a pang. It was for the pure unstained honour of his home he trembled; his heart ached, and his soul seemed stretched upon a rack of agony. Strange thoughts and thick-coming fancies crowded upon his brain. He heard the voice of time ring out from the old church steeple, and tell him in solemn muffled tones that the hours were flying, each one bringing nearer and nearer the catastrophe he dreaded. The spectre, Guilt, would soon be on the threshold of that peaceful home, trampling down the pride of generations, and throwing over all the blush of shame and dishonour. Could nothing be done to avert the evil? The clock struck one. He rose from his seat, threw open his window, and looked out upon the night; there was not a star to be seen; all without was gloomy and mysterious—dark as the night within his own soul. He leaned out, and let the cold wind blow upon his feverish temples, and wander through his hair, fresh and cool to his brain. By degrees his mood changed and softened; he woke up from the blindness of despair, and looked with sorrow on the past, as well as terror on the future. In a moment (as a flash of lightning might have broken through the leaden sky, and lighted up with a sudden flash the surrounding prospect, rendering every object distinctly visible) he saw every act of sin or folly he had committed, from his earliest days till now, at a single glance—a dreary prospect it was. He saw the evil that was, the good that might have been, and he mourned bitterly over the ruins of his wasted life. Oh! for one chance—one trial more! Had the stream of Fate set dead against him? or might he by one adroit stroke avoid the breakers ahead?—for a time, at least. A thought struck him—a thought that made his heart beat, and sent the blood leaping violently through his veins. A drowning man will clutch at a straw, unheeding whither that straw will waft him, whether it will eventually save, or only delay his doom; he is content to be saved, if it is only for an hour. Some such feeling as this filled Laurence's mind, as he caught eagerly at the hope that was to save him from ruin. In the daylight he would have shunned it, as he might have shunned any other hideous thing that crossed his path; but in the gloom and darkness of the night, he took it to his heart and dallied with it, till he became so familiarized with the thought that the act seemed easy. His mind was confused; right and wrong were so blended together, that he could scarce tell one from the other. There was no time for deliberation; no time for reflection. What he intended to do must be done at once. He quickly persuaded himself that adding wrong to wrong was the nearest approach to right, that Fate left him power to accomplish. The ghost of a smile, like a gleam of his old reckless self, flickered across his face as he lighted his lamp, and prepared to descend the stairs. He opened his door, and cast a keen cautious glance out upon the landing, and up and down the stairs to see if any signs of life were stirring. No, all was still and silent as the grave. Slowly he descended, pausing at every step; listening, almost fearing to breathe, lest the sound of his own breathing should awake the sleepers. He looked like a moving monument of fear, as he crept stealthily along till he reached the Rector's study. He entered it and closed the door behind him. Light in hand he approached the escritoire, and examined the lock. He saw at a glance that it would be very difficult to open without a regular picklock. He must force it open.

He went into the servants'-hall, and searched till he found a small screw-driver; this he carried back to the study, used it as a lever, and with all his force proceeded to his degrading task.

Crack! the wood was yielding. The slight sharp noise it made sounded in his ear like thunder. He paused a second, and trembled in every limb. The perspiration stood like beads upon his forehead; it was no use to hesitate now; he had gone too far to recede—he must persevere to the end; he could not go back. He bent forward to his task once more, turned his hand—crack! he touched the lid, and the escritoire flew open! He looked down for a second, horrified at what he had done. He felt as though he had committed the worst of sacrileges, in thus forcing his way to the private records of his father's life—the temple of his thoughts—the chronicle of his days. The Rector's papers were all arranged with great care and order. His diary—his correspondence—his thought-book, and miscellaneous memoranda, lay exposed at the first opening of the desk. These were nothing to Laurence; he pushed them on one side, and proceeded anxiously to search for what he expected to find. One thing after another he tossed restlessly aside. From the back of one drawer he drew out a mass of papers. He shook the fluttering sheets eagerly, and out from among them fell a long light tress of curling hair! As the silken rings twined round his trembling fingers, it seemed as though they were thick cords tightening round his heartstrings.

He almost cried out aloud as he recognised
and shook off the shining threads, which he
had once seen clustering round his mother's
living face. The sight of that sacred relic of
the dead gave him a terrible shock. There
was an atmosphere of the grave around it.
He shivered as though a cold hand had been
stretched out from that grave, and laid lov-
ingly, warningly upon him to arrest his progress further.

For a moment he was overcome; but the first
feeling of superstitious awe soon crumbled away
before the strong pressure of the necessity which
he believed brought him there. He proceeded
pertinaciously with his task. Patiently and per-
severingly he ransacked one place after another,
without success. His heart sank within him;
what if he had added this act of domestic
treachery to his other sins, and it availed him
nothing? Presently, when he had almost aban-
doned himself to despair, his hand clasped a
crisp roll of papers. He knew, by the feeling,

they were banknotes, and every pulse throbbed with joy, as he clutched and drew them from their hiding-place. He was not deceived. He smoothed them out one after the other. There were more than enough for his self-redemption. He selected just sufficient to redeem the paper from the hands of the crafty lawyer. He would not have touched a penny more even to save himself from starving. He replaced the superfluous notes, and grasped the others firmly, as though he feared they would disappear from his sight. He regarded them as the means of his salvation. He felt as though this one last wrong would set his world right. He would never, never sin again. A hundred strong resolves came rushing through his brain. He felt like a man who had received a sudden reprieve from a fate worse than death; he uttered one long deep-drawn sigh of relief. Suddenly there fell over him a feeling that he was not alone. He fancied his sigh was softly repeated. Slowly, and in unutterable dread, he turned his eyes round the room. There, in the darkened doorway, stood Mrs. Carlton, as white as the dressing-robe she had hastily flung over her. She stepped into the room, and closed the door softly behind her. Laurence neither moved nor spoke, but kept his eyes fixed upon her with an expression of blank, bewildered shame. She dropped her eyes from his face to the open escritoire, thence to the roll of notes he still held within his hand. She saw and comprehended *all*.

"Oh! Laurence, has it come to this?"

There was more of grievous surprise than anger or reproach in her tone. Her face was exceedingly sorrowful, and her eyes rested pityingly upon him. He was touched to the quick, utterly overcome, but a few words faltered from his cold white lips.

"It is for my father's sake!"

An angry flush overspread her cheek, as she said quickly,

"How! for your *father's sake,* you come on such an errand as this?"

Half in answer to her, half as though pursuing his own thoughts, he added—

"I would bear it all, if I could bear it alone!"

The blank misery of his tones, the despairing expression of his face, chilled Mrs. Carlton's blood. There was something more than the weight of a young man's folly on his conscience, something involving his family. Perhaps ruin to him, and woe to them. She stepped lightly to his side, laid one hand upon his shoulder, and said in a low, impressive whisper,

"What is it, Laurence? Don't be afraid, I will be a mother to you if I can—trust me."

Trust her! yes, he would trust her. She was his father's wife, and would have mercy on her husband's son. He looked on her still, eloquent face, and felt that in all the world he could find no fitter confidante, no surer friend, than the noble-minded woman by his side. Briefly, humbly, and repentantly, he told her all ; extenuating nothing, excusing nothing, he laid the bare truth before her. He did not look in her face as he was speaking, but turned his eyes away from very shame. He ceased. She too was silent. His pulse quickened. How had his recital affected her? Why did she not speak, say something to express her feelings? Anything would be better than this silence, this suspense. He stole a glance towards her. She had thrown herself into a chair, and was sitting in stony stillness, her hands folded in her lap, her head bent down, her lips compressed. Her whole attitude was that of concentrated thought. She sighed heavily at last, and looked up in his face; she saw that he had suffered, and suffered deeply. There was no virtuous indignation, nor refined upbraiding in her voice or manner, as she said,

"This is indeed a grievous story, Laurence; your father—" Alarmed at the mention of his name, Laurence interrupted her, saying almost fiercely—

"My father! I have confessed to you; you will not betray me to him?"

"Do you think I would break my husband's heart?" she answered quickly; "no, I will not betray you to him. He shall never know from me how you have fallen—never! That secret must rest between us two."

"Thank God!—thank God!" he exclaimed, clasping her hands with both his own. "You will help me to keep it." He paused a second, then added, pointing to the broken escritoire. "It is better my father should think he is robbed by a stranger, than know he has been thus dishonoured by his son—dishonoured, not for a day, but for all time. It would kill him!"

"Yes," said Mrs. Carlton, shuddering, "it would be horrible! A Carlton arraigned for forgery and robbery! Oh! Laurence, how could you——"

"Ay, how could I?" he said, with passionate grief; "how could I commit a hundred follies every day of my life?—and, Heaven knows, I may commit a hundred more."

"God forbid!—I pray that you may die first!" exclaimed Mrs. Carlton.

"Amen!" he said fervently. Observing that her eyes were fixed upon the notes, he held them towards her, saying,

"Count them—I have taken just enough to redeem my bill—no more." She took them from his hand, and replaced them with the rest, saying,

"This is your father's money—it must not be touched; you have given me your confidence, and I will be your friend, not your accomplice, Laurence. I could not be cognisant of such an act as this, and remain silent."

"What must I do?"

"Let me think," she answered. "It is a large sum to be forthcoming at a moment's notice." After a moment's reflection, she added, "I will see and speak with the man Jorley to-morrow."

"It is useless," said Laurence; "he will have no mercy."

"I should not ask for any," she answered. "You can soon pack your valise, and start with him for London to-morrow. I will give you a letter of introduction to my brother. When you present that, he will at once give you a check for the amount you require."

A few broken words were all that Laurence could utter—his heart was too full—no language could adequately have expressed his feelings.

Mrs. Carlton made no attempt to lecture or to sermonize on the wickedness he had committed. She saw that he felt his position keenly. No words of hers could have heightened his sense of his present degradation, or have strengthened his resolution for the future. She was too generous to take advantage of the fallen, or to trample on one who was already crushed and wounded enough. She reserved her forces, and when the right time came, would open fire with good effect. Her kind forbearance affected him more, far more, than the thunders of a moralist would have done. When he retired to his room that night, he felt as though the past events had been a dream—a mass of unsubstantial shadows; and as the day dawned upon the outer world, the opening of a brighter and a better life seemed to dawn upon his soul.

CHAPTER VIII.

POOR NEP!

" O mother, yet no mother,
Mother—miscalled—farewell !"

LIFE at the Manor-house crept onward
with a slow, crawling pace, stealing
away the hours and days of Adrienne's youth,
making her cheek pale, and her heart heavy,
for want of sympathy. Her spirit sickened and
drooped for that sunshine of the soul which
never penetrated to her gloomy home. She
would sit for hours looking languidly from
her window, watching the autumn tints stealing over the green trees, wondering if life
brought to all the world such bitter fruit as

it brought to her. The one bright spot in her life had clouded over. Her visits to the Rectory, though not exactly prohibited, were discontinued, in consequence of her having borrowed a volume of Scott's poems from Grace, and being discovered reading them aloud to Mathilde. Unfortunately for Adrienne, the scene she had chosen for her sister's edification or amusement, was the trial and condemnation of Constance, in the poem of Marmion.

Madame de Fontaine was passing the open window at the time. Attracted by Adri-. enne's impassioned, impressive voice, she listened, and heard the unhappy Constance denounce her judges, her destroyers. Poetry was at all times obnoxious to Madame de Fontaine's ears. The gracefully flowing verse, the sublime thought, the vivid coloring that falls on common things, making the old seem new, throwing over all a glory and a charm unspeakable—all was lost upon her. She could not appreciate the lights and shadows of the poet's genius, nor recognise the spirit of beauty that brightened his song. She regarded it as the excrescence of an idle, profitless life, calculated only to mislead or bewilder the mind. " Marmion" was especially distasteful to Madame de Fontaine. Her anger knew no bounds, when, on entering the room, she discovered Mathilde listening with a kind of rapt fascination, while her sister read ; in her excitement she had partially raised herself from her couch, and with clasped hands, intent eyes, and parted lips, drank in eagerly the tale that told of love, ruin, and despair. It was the first time she had ever tasted the forbidden fruit of legendary lore. The magic beauty of it held her spell-bound, as by an enchanter's wand. Who shall say the days of enchantment are over, while the essence of a dead man's spirit still circulates through the world, working the same mysteries, wringing tears from the eyes, awakening the sympathies of the heart from generation to generation?

The sisters were so deeply enthralled with the poem, the one reading, the other listening, that they were wholly unconscious that the audience was increased, until Madame de Fontaine's shadow fell over them. Mathilde, affrighted, sank back upon her couch, and covered her face as though she had been caught in the commission of a deadly sin. Adrienne shook back the hair that had fallen over her eyes, the remnants of those once luxuriant tresses, and smiled in her mother's face, saying,

"You there, mamma! What a pity! if you had only come half an hour ago, you might have heard it all."

"I have heard enough," began Madame de Fontaine, her face darkening.

"Ah, but you have no idea how beautifully it goes on," exclaimed Adrienne, interrupting her; "they bury her alive! because she is human, and has felt human love, human sin, and human sorrow. They give her no hope of mercy here or hereafter—they abuse, insult, and bury her alive! the cruel cowards! Oh, if I were a God, how I would judge those men!"

"Hold your blasphemous tongue!" exclaimed Madame de Fontaine, startled out of her usual cold self-possession. "See how right I am in forbidding those lying romances in my house! You take them for truth, and poison with the pernicious lie your sister's soul, that has been trained for higher, holier things."

"Mother, forgive me!" exclaimed Mathilde, her pale face expressive of deep sorrow, "the fault is all mine. I was as ready to listen as she was to read. God forgive me!"

. "Amen!" said Madame de Fontaine, devoutly. "Your disobedience to me is nothing, compared with your disobedience to your Church. Father Dominic must deal with that. But you have both acted in defiance of my domestic authority, and that is my concern. Give me the book, and go to your room, Adrienne."

Adrienne felt she had done wrong in obeying her first impulse to irritate her mother. She was sorry for it now, more for her sister's sake than for her own. The flush faded from her face, and she said, almost humbly,

"The book is not mine, mamma, I cannot give it to you. I am very sorry to have vexed you; but if you will forgive Mathilde, I will promise never to open the book again." Her mother made no answer, but stretched out her hand and took the book. She saw Grace Carlton's name written on the fly-leaf.

"I thought the acquaintance of your heretical friends would lead to no good," she remarked.

"It has led to no harm," said Adrienne, arming herself for their defence.

Madame de Fontaine allowed her to proceed no farther. She was only too glad to have an opportunity of censuring the Carltons, whom in her heart she detested; her dislike to them increased as they progressed in Adrienne's affection. There was no denying the fact that the wild spirit which Madame de Fontaine, with all her parental authority, was unable to subdue, was to the Carltons all gentleness and affection. Their influence over her was too apparent to be overlooked; she was to them more docile and submissive than to her mother—more patient of rebuke, less inclined to retort. Adrienne's evident improvement, instead of gratifying, irritated Madame de Fontaine; she preferred the evil that might result from her own work, rather than that good which was the result of another's assistance. She knew the Carltons had cast a charm over Adrienne's life, and, like the bad fairy in the children's stories, she longed to destroy it. She seized the opportunity now afforded her, saying—

"No harm!—is it no harm to sow discord and dissension where there should be peace? —no harm to put in your hands the means not only of injuring your own soul, but of spreading the poison, and contaminating those around you! Look at Mathilde!—she who has vowed to avoid all light works and conversation, has been tempted not only to break her vow, but to hear her religion reviled—its professors held up to scorn."

"Blame and punish me, mamma, as much as you please," pleaded Adrienne, "but don't be angry with Mathilde. It was no fault of hers. I coaxed her, and made her listen to me. Her life is so sad and dreary, I wanted her to know what beautiful things men have thought and written."

"Your ideas of beauty are different to mine," said Madame de Fontaine; "I shall return this volume to the Rectory, and in future shall give them fewer opportunities of pandering to your vitiated taste. I have always had my misgivings as to the prudence of your intimacy there. Now I am determined it shall cease."

Adrienne was overwhelmed with grief. She tried in vain to shake her mother's resolution. Then, failing in that, she submitted patiently to her decree, trusting that, if her anger were left unopposed, it would gradually die out, and permission to visit the Rectory would again be granted. Days passed; Adrienne behaved with extraordinary sweetness and docility, but Madame de Fontaine gave no signs of yielding. Once Adrienne ventured to touch upon the subject, but her advances met with such decided opposition, that she saw at once it was vain to hope, at present, for any change in favour of her friends. She felt heart-sick and weary; she wrote a long letter to Lena, explaining matters, and despatched it by her trusty messenger, Nep. She hardly dared to expect, yet she half hoped to receive an answer. She knew that Mrs. Carlton would strongly object to any correspondence being carried on without the knowledge, and against the express wish of Madame de Fontaine. Adrienne posted herself at the window, and watched Neptune trotting soberly across the meadows, as though fully impressed with the importance of his mission. Presently she saw him returning at a slow solemn pace, with ears laid back and drooping tail, as though he knew he was bringing back no welcome news to his young mistress, and did not care to hurry himself. There was no letter, but round his neck was tied a bunch of flowers, which told her she was sweetly remembered. For some days, indeed, since she had given her sister the literary entertainment of "Marmion," she had not seen Mathilde. This did not particularly surprise her, as Mathilde was frequently confined to her room for days together, not entirely from ill-health, but in pursuance of her studies, or in the performance of her religious duties. It was almost a week since they had met, when Adrienne encountered her sister creeping languidly down the stairs, looking pale and ill. In a moment Adrienne was at her side, full of tender anxiety and care.

"How ill you look, Mathilde! What have you been doing all this time? You think and study too much—and what is the good of it all? Weak and suffering as you always

are, you will kill yourself if you go on like
this."

She threw her arms round Mathilde's neck,
and almost shook her with impulsive fondness.
Mathilde made no reply, but after a moment's
pause, gently unclasped the hands from about
her neck, kissed them, and put them from her.
Adrienne, surprised at the gesture, looked inquiringly in her sister's face, and noticed the
tears gathering slowly in her eyes.

"Have I done anything to vex you, Mathilde? Are you angry with me? Why don't
you speak? You know I would not do anything to grieve you for all the world."

Mathilde placed her finger on her lips, and
attempted to pass on. Adrienne fancied she
was afraid they would be overheard. She
looked cautiously round; there was no one
near; she lowered her tone as she added—

"Come into my room; we can talk there as
much as we please."

Mathilde again, with a sad look of peculiar

intelligence, placed her finger 'on her lips. Adrienne's eyes positively blazed with anger.

"What!" she exclaimed. "Have they forbidden you to speak to me? I see how it is. They know the one, the only grain of human love they have left in your heart is mine, and they want to rob me of it." Again she twined her arms round her sister's neck. "They know we love one another, Mathilde, and they want to part us. It is cruel—it is wicked—I have lost my friends now, and, from day to day, have nothing to live for, nothing to love, but you—Mathilde—speak to me, sister, do speak."

Mathilde held her closely folded in her arms, pressed her cold clammy lips upon her sister's blooming cheek, but remained silent, and, but for the one movement, still, like a statue of breathing marble.

"Why do you cling to such a cruel creed?" added Adrienne, in a voice broken and full of sorrow. "You grow paler and paler every day —they are killing you—they are trying to stamp out every living feeling within you. Oh! why——"

Before she could finish her sentence, Mathilde, with one rapid movement, unclasped her arms, put her away from her, and hurried down the stairs. Adrienne's heart swelled, and a passionate flood of tears relieved her. She grieved bitterly over her separation from her sister, and felt doubly alone. From this time they met only at mealtimes; but the vow of silence was rigidly kept up. The want of congenial occupation, the solitary life she led, the utter absence of anything likely to amuse or instruct a young enthusiastic spirit, began to tell on Adrienne's health. The bloom faded from her cheeks, and a fiery flush, like the glow of an intermittent fever, took its place; indeed, a kind of intermittent fever crept into her life. Occasionally her wild spirits would blaze forth with something of their natural fire; at another time she would feel languid and depressed, and would burst into tears, with no perceptible cause. Music, her great solace, she could no longer enjoy. The piano was closed to her; the sound of it irritated Madame de Fontaine's nerves. But she had no power to stop the music that would sometimes burst from Adrienne's soul. She would sit for hours together, with folded arms, her eyes gazing out dreamily from her window, and pour out her whole soul in song. The rich melodious music would swell from her slender throat, now like a cry of indignation, then quivering and changing to a wail of sorrow, like the plaintive moan of a stricken, wounded thing. Once when she had been singing thus, as though she would sing her life away, her eyes brightened suddenly— she saw Grace and Lena crossing the meadows, she leaned from her window, and sang still louder. She fancied they heard her, for they stopped and listened, then looked up to her window, and returned her salutation.

From that time, every day at the same hour, she placed herself at the window, and watched and waited to see them pass. It often happened that they failed to come that way; then her disappointment was bitter in the extreme—none but those who have been situated like herself could understand how such bitter grief could rise from so trivial a cause. The mere sight of them, as they passed along, was to her as welcome as the ray of light or breath of air is to the poor prisoner who spends his life in gloom and darkness.

Occasionally, however, she would vary the monotony of her life by getting into some domestic scrape, scaring her mother's major-domo almost out of his wits; which was no difficult task, for he was not burthened with many. Born and bred in an obscure hamlet in the south of France, he had inherited all the small superstitions natural enough to the uneducated classes of all ages; combined with these, he had a pious horror of all heretics, and an unbounded faith in the virtues of his mistress, Madame de Fontaine. He had also a kind of compassionate regard for Adrienne; her youth, beauty, and loneliness touched the old man's heart, and he almost forgot she was a heretic, till some strange trick reminded him of the fact.

One morning he was horrified at finding a caricature of Father Dominic, Madame de Fontaine's great friend and spiritual director. The reverend gentleman was represented as making a vigorous attack on the follies of his neighbours, while a host of petty sins and vices were quietly creeping under his cassock on one side, turning out charity, patience, and many minor virtues on the other. François crossed himself, and carried the trophy off to his mistress. Adrienne was severely reprimanded, and rather enjoyed the excitement her production occasioned, than otherwise. At the present time she owed a grudge to Father Dominic, for she believed it to be through his influence that Mathilde was undergoing the penance of silence. One morning, as she returned from a listless wander through the garden, she observed the Father's hat and cloak in the hall. She was ripe for mischief; a thought struck her, and she laughed gleefully at the idea. As Father Dominic's visits were always limited, she knew almost to a moment when he would leave the house. Before that time arrived, she displaced a statue of St. Joseph which decorated the hall, pressed Neptune into her service, and placed him on the pedestal instead. She next proceeded to dress him in the reverend gentleman's hat and cloak; then, as a crowning point, she put in his mouth a short pipe, which she had ransacked all corners of the house to find.

Having sufficiently instructed Nep in his duty, she relieved him, and changed his position, lest he should get tired, and fail to "stand at ease," when the right moment came. Presently she heard the library door open; then she knew that they were coming. She whispered her last instructions to Nep, bid him "hold fast—stand firm." He wagged his tail, and blinked his soft brown eyes, as much as to say he was quite up to the joke. Adrienne then retired behind a curtain, where she could see without being seen. With her slow, stately tread, Madame de Fontaine accompanied her visitor to the door. On reaching the hall she raised her eyes. Her cheek flushed, and her eyes gleamed as they fell, first on the fallen saint, then on Adrienne's favourite, who occupied his place.

"I am sorry you should be insulted in my house, Father," she said, and her voice trembled slightly. "I will see to this."

"No matter, Madame," replied the old man, gently. "I cannot think this was intended for an insult. Those who do not respect the saints, would consider this merely as a jest, and nothing more."

As he spoke, he stretched out his hand to take his hat and cloak, but Nep gave a low growl.

"Do not touch him," exclaimed Madame de Fontaine. "It is a malignant beast; the hand that set him up must take him down, he will permit no other to do it. I know his vicious temper of old."

She divined, and rightly, that Adrienne was not far off, and, without raising her voice, uttered her daughter's name, "Adrienne," and waited for her to come. Adrienne had expected a burst of indignation from her mother, and that some envenomed bitterness would flow from the Father's lips. Her mother's manner deceived, and the Father's exculpatory words amazed her. She felt embarrassed and ashamed, and came out blushing from her hiding-place. Slowly, without a word on either side, with flushed cheeks and eyes cast down, she disrobed the dog, and handed the hat and cloak to Father Dominic. Nay, more, she helped to put on the cloak.

"Child, it was a foolish trick," he said, with a mild accent of reproach. "It is a bad sign

for the young to irreverence old age. According-
ing to your own faith, it is a sin God himself
has rebuked."

"I am very sorry—I beg your pardon," said
Adrienne, in a subdued, low voice.

"The very best or the very worst of us can
do no more than acknowledge a fault," he said,
"and avoid it for the future. One word before
we part, young lady," he added. "You sully
the purity of your own faith when you outrage
that of another; remember you should never be
tempted to jest at that which another holds
sacred."

He reinstated St. Joseph in his place, crossed
himself, and left the house. Adrienne glanced
up in her mother's face, and, culprit like, expected that as soon as Father Dominic had
departed, she should receive a severe reprimand.
She was mistaken. Madame de Fontaine
spoke not a word, but went direct to her own
room.

Adrienne caught a momentary glimpse of

her face as she crossed the hall; its expression
puzzled her. Madame de Fontaine had neither
spoken nor acted like an indignant person, or
like one seriously enraged; to Adrienne she
had not uttered even a word of censure; but
yet there was a look of settled satisfied fury in
her eye, a spot of fire on her cheek, as though
she had arranged and executed a work of vengeance—yet she uttered not a word! Adrienne
congratulated herself upon her escape, and fancied her foolish frolic was forgiven. She little
thought that a scheme of vengeance, cold, cruel,
and deadly, was being rapidly arranged in her
mother's subtle brain—a scheme that would
drench her soul with sorrow and her eyes with
tears.

The day passed away slowly. Mother and
daughters met at dinner. Mathilde, so Adrienne
supposed, was absolved from her vow; her penance was over. She seemed more cheerful,
and talked much more than was habitually her
custom. A glow of genial warmth seemed to

be gradually creeping to Adrienne's heart, as she nestled close to her elder sister's side. Dinner was over. François was solemnly clearing the table, when they were all startled by the sound of a pistol-shot, which seemed to have been fired close to the house. Madame de Fontaine glanced across the table at Adrienne, and a quiet satisfied smile parted her lips. She made no inquiry, uttered no remark. A strange, unfathomable feeling crept over Adrienne's spirit. She turned hot and cold in the same moment—she feared something terrible, though her fears had no tangible shape.

"What is that noise, mamma? What can it mean?" she asked, and she turned colder still.

"It means that *you* have one plaything less, and *I* have lost an enemy," replied Madame de Fontaine.

With one wild cry, or rather shriek, Adrienne started up, dashed open the window,

and sprang out. She cared nothing for the
wind or the rain that beat into her face, and
ran trickling down her bare neck and shoulders. Swift as a youug fawn she flew across
the garden, calling in an agonized voice,
"Nep! Nep!" as she ran. There was no answer. At the entrance to the first meadow
she saw a sorry sight. The under-gardener,
a north-country lad, was dragging along the
ground the bleeding body of her faithful favourite.

"Oh! Nep!—Nep!" she cried in an agony
of grief, as she flung herself down, and threw
her arms round the still breathing, fast dying
creature; "you loved me, and they have
killed you!"

The sound of her voice recalled the poor
dog to life. He struggled to get up on his
legs, but fell; and as he lay upon the ground,
turned his filmy eyes, with a last loving look of
recognition, on her face, and tried to lick her
hand, but his mouth was filled with blood. His

limbs quivered and stiffened, while his glazed eyes were still fixed upon her face; but the light had left them—they would never brighten at the sound of her voice again—poor Nep was dead!

His young mistress bent over him in speechless sorrow. He had been her trusty friend and companion for so many years of her joyless life, that his dumb companionship seemed necessary to her existence. She had been used to talk to him as she could talk to no other living thing —tell him all her troubles, and the secret of all her hopes and fears. She fancied he comprehended her language, and felt that his wise brown eyes looked all the sympathy he had not the power to express. Now he was dead—he had been cruelly killed through her! Her foolish frolic, like many other trifling things, had been fraught with weighty consequences; it had brought death to him, sorrow to her. She felt as though something good and pure had been taken out of her life, that would never come

back to it again. She crouched beside the poor
dead thing she had loved so well, and sobbed as
though her heart would break.

"Missis said it wur dangerous mad, and had
best be put out o' the way sharp," said the lad,
touched by her grief.

"Take care of him, Jem, get some clean hay,
and put him in the stable," said Adrienne,
rousing herself.

"So I will, Miss, never fear; though I wur
told to dig a hole and bury him."

As Adrienne re-entered the house, she encountered her mother. Both were pale. They
gazed steadily at each other. It was Adrienne
who spoke.

"This has been a bitter blow, mother; but
it's the last—the last you shall strike at me,"
and she passed swiftly up the stairs.

CHAPTER IX.

PERPLEXED IN THE EXTREME.

" Child, dry thine eyes! a day will come at last
When present grief lies buried in the past.
Hold up thine head! go forward brave and strong,
The way is weary, but it lasts not long."

AT noon, the day following Mrs. Carlton's midnight interview with Laurence,
a letter was handed to the Rector, as he sat
in his study with his wife. He glanced at
the superscription, and saw that it was in the
handwriting of his son. "What could Laurence have to write about?" he wondered,
"when he was living in the house, and could
have spoken to him any hour of the day."
He hesitated; he was evidently in no hurry

to learn what the letter contained. He had a
dark thought in his mind; perhaps he dreaded
lest that letter might contain the confirmation
of his fears. His hand shook slightly as he
opened it. He read it to the end in attentive
silence. Mrs. Carlton kept her eyes fixed, with
a kind of guilty consciousness, upon her work.
She was perfectly acquainted with the contents
of the letter; but, with well-assumed ignorance,
waited for her husband to speak. Mr. Carlton,
looking up, said,

"So Laurence has gone, Christina."

"Gone!" she answered, letting her work
fall, and waiting as though for farther information.

"He gives me no explanation of a matter
that he knows has perplexed me greatly," said
the Rector, gloomily. "He says nothing of his
intentions, nor of his plans for the future. He
merely tells me that he is weary of the dull,
inactive life he leads, is sorry for all the anxiety
he has caused me, and he engages that the

future shall atone for the past. Hear what he says." Mr. Carlton read aloud the last paragraph: "I have not yet made up my mind as to what path I shall take; but, rest assured, you shall have an honourable account of me, or you shall never hear of me again."

"Words! mere words!" exclaimed the Rector, as he threw down the letter.

"You must not look on the gloomy side—I have great hopes of him," said Mrs. Carlton.

"So had I once," sighed the Rector; "but one by one they have all been blighted. I can hope no longer."

"But you must not despair," she answered; "for my part, I have faith in his promise now, and I believe he will struggle hard to keep it."

"If he succeeds, it will be for the first time in his life," said the Rector, with the acerbity of a man who has often been bitterly disappointed.

" We are not all made strong alike, Edward,"
said Mrs. Carlton, eager to put in an extenuat‑
ing word for the absent one.   " Remember, it
is easier for some than for others to resist
temptation.   Where a strong mind can with‑
stand it, a weaker one will fall.   Laurence
has been a great trouble to you, I know; his
nature is one ᶜ those gay, volatile combina‑
tions, full of ephemera. follies, easily affected by
every passing circumstance.   Unfortunately, he
is what is called a merry companion, full of
life and good spirits; he has no doubt been
very much sought after by a class of fast
young men as wild and reckless as himself.
He has had too much of those pleasures which
lead to pain.   I think he sees his folly now;
you, too, will see him change for the better.
As he grows older, his principles will grow
stronger, and his purpose become more fixed.
Mark my words, Edward, you will live to be
proud of your son yet."

" God grant it !" said the Rector, fervently;

"you speak so hopefully, you almost inspire me with hope. Sometimes, Christina, I fancy you think I have been hard upon the lad."

"No, not hard," she answered; "but I do not think you have ever understood each other. There are some subtle chords in human nature difficult to tune, and most delicate to touch; I do not think it is in a man's power to find them, either in his own sex or in ours. With all the will to do right," she added, smiling, "you men make sad blunders. I think you and Laurence have been playing at cross purposes; your dispositions are so different; his thoughts have never blended with yours; but I do not think you have been hard with him. You have been sorely tried, no doubt."

The Rector sat for some moments silent, shading his eyes, according to his habit when buried in painful thought. He was still haunted by the suspicion that his son was cognizant of, if not connected with, the outrage that had been contemplated against him that fearful night

in the meadows. He certainly had good grounds
for the suspicion, having discovered Laurence in
close conversation with one of the gang the
day following the occurrence. Yet, in spite of
appearances, he could not reconcile himself to
the thought that his son was guilty. It would
be too terrible, if true. He tried to chase
the idea from his mind; but it came back
again and again with redoubled strength. He
could not shake it off. By a single act of
confidence, Laurence might have put himself
right with his father; but he did not; he remained obstinate when he should have been
obedient. Now he was gone. There was no
chance of speaking to him face to face, and all
hope of having the matter cleared up was ended.

The Rector had never mentioned his meeting
with Laurence and Jem Dawkes, on that me-
morable morning, even to his wife. He did not
like to dwell too much on his son's vices, even
to her. Now, as they sat together alone, he
told her all the facts, as well as his own sur-

mises thereupon. Learning this, Mrs. Carlton
better understood why Laurence had refused to
make his father acquainted with his position;
under existing circumstances, his doing so might
have heightened the suspicion that already clung
to him. She utterly repudiated the idea of his
being guilty of anything beyond reckless extravagance and folly. She spoke well and
earnestly in his defence, showing in how many
different ways he might have been brought in
contact with his father's would-be assailants, and
yet in no way cognizant of their conspiracy
against him; until the Rector began to look on
the matter with her eyes, and the possibility of
his son's innocence became, for the time being,
more probable to him.

"Another circumstance, besides his abrupt
departure, has unnerved me this morning," said
the Rector. "About half an hour ago, just before you came in to sit with me, I had occasion
to go to my escritoire, and found the lock had
been forced."

"Well!" exclaimed Mrs. Carlton, quite taken aback at this announcement; for in her anxiety about Laurence she had forgotten that the Rector could not fail to discover the fact that the escritoire had been forced.

"Strange to say," he added, "the contents are all safe, nothing seems to have been meddled with—at least, so far as I have at present discovered. My money, the only thing that would tempt a thief, is safe; but I must make inquiries, for whoever forced my desk must have had an object in doing so."

"If I were you, Edward, since you have lost nothing, I would let the matter rest as it is," said Mrs. Carlton.

"I cannot do that," he answered; "I should never feel safe. I must find, or try to find out who has committed this outrage. If any of the outer bolts or bars had been forced, we should have heard of it. It is therefore evident that some inmate of the house is guilty, and I am determined to discover who. Although I have lost nothing, it is monstrous to have my locks broken, and my private affairs investigated by prying eyes. There must have been some motive for the act. It is unfortunate that this should have happened just on the day that Laurence has chosen to depart."

"It is for that very reason I advise you to make no stir," said Mrs. Carlton anxiously; "you know Laurence bears no very brilliant character in the village; his follies have been bruited abroad, and he is considered a kind of 'ne'er-do-well.' Now he has disappeared, and your desk has been broken open, these two facts united might give rise to the rumour that your son had robbed you and absconded! Think if such a scandal should get reported, how humiliating it would be for us; how cruel to him, if innocent!"

"What you say may be all very true, Christina," replied Mr. Carlton; "I admit the full force of your argument, but still I cannot consent to sit down quietly and let such an act pass unnoticed. I shall be in a constant state of suspicious irritation till I find out who has been guilty of this felonious act."

"But, Edward," said Mrs. Carlton, earnestly—"don't start at what I am going to say. Suppose it should really be Laurence who is the guilty party? Guilty, I say, and yet not guilty. Do you remember having told me that, as a boy, Laurence used to walk in his sleep? and sometimes conceal his sister's toys and his own, in the most unheard of places. Is it impossible that the fit may have again seized him, and led him to do this? Nothing is lost—your papers are not even disarranged. Who in their right senses would have committed such a motiveless act, as to force a desk and leave the contents untouched?"

Mrs. Carlton talked and argued till her husband had partially adopted her view of the matter. However, he was still greatly discomposed at the abrupt departure of his son. He was harassed by a thousand anxious fears.

Perhaps he was not quite satisfied that his own conduct had been of the most judicious character, in reference to his son. A shadow of self-reproach mingled with his thoughts as he recalled their last interview. He fancied that if he had himself been more sympathetic and patient, Laurence would have been more open and confiding. Now, looking back on the years that were past, it seemed to him that many of the differences which had arisen, and become stumbling-blocks between them, might have been smoothed and surmounted. He had used the curb, when he might have held the snaffle, and the spur when he should have used the guiding-rein. But when are either men or women wise at the right time? It is difficult for the physician to discover the right treatment for the sick body, although he has the result of the experience of thousands who have preceded him; how much more difficult it is to find the right treatment of a sore in that spiritual part of us which rules all our thoughts and actions. It is no easy task to train the unseen spirit in the right and healthy way of life. We have no outer clue to guide us through its hidden ways and windings, and are too apt to be deceived by appearances, which too often conceal that which with so much loving earnestness we are seeking. To us all—to the ignorant as well as to the wise—sooner or later, the charge of a human soul is committed, and it is an awful responsibility to possess. Every word, every act—indeed, every thought, may have some influence, for good or for evil, over the life of another. Those who love us best may unwittingly lay the foundation-stone on which is raised a vast fabric of misconstruction. From loving lips there sometimes falls the first drop of bitterness, which spreads and widens till it becomes a river rolling between us. As years pass on, we stand on different sides, and wonder how we became thus divided. From small misunderstandings come great sunderings.

If Mr. Carlton and his son could have stood spiritually face to face—had each seen the heart of the other—matters would have been different. But they had looked only into each other's eyes, and had been deceived; they had spoken, and had been misled. The son had gone away with a vexed and wounded spirit; the father remained at home, regretful, and full of vague rankling suspicions that would not be plucked out.

The Rector went about his daily duties; in relieving the sorrows and condoling with the misfortunes of others, he found some attenuation of his own troubles; he returned home in the evening in a more cheerful frame of mind. Seeing that he had partially recovered his usual spirits, Mrs. Carlton fancied he was inclined to look on the brighter side respecting his son's departure. She was herself quite satisfied that, as soon as he was in her brother's hands, all would be well with Laurence. She was most anxious to satisfy her husband's mind, so far as she could; but she put a constraint on herself, lest she might say too much, or lead him to suspect she knew more than she chose to avow. So long as she was silent, all was safe. But a word of hers might lead on from one question or remark to another, to the revelation of that scene which she was most anxious to conceal.

As the evening closed in, dreary and dark, with a drizzling rain and cold biting wind, he went to the window, and remained there looking out for some moments in silence. There was a great contrast between the bright aspect of things within the house and the dreariness without. There was no moon—not a star to be seen. Above was one canopy of leaden clouds, shadowing the earth in gloom and darkness. Presently he turned from the window; he seemed to forget his girls were in the room, for he sighed heavily, and said—

"I may have been hard upon my boy in small matters, but he is harder still on me to-night." He was evidently deeply agitated, as he added: "It is terrible to think that he may be wandering, penniless, friendless, and alone on such a night as this. God knows what will become of him!"

"Why, papa, what do you mean? Has Laurie gone away?"

Mrs. Carlton hastened to explain matters to them, saying,

"Yes, he has gone away, and your father is very uneasy about him. He has left home and gone to London, without giving us any notice of his intentions, or leaving any address behind him."

"Is that all?" exclaimed Grace; "for my part, I wonder he has stayed at home so long."

"Why are you so especially anxious about him, papa?" asked Lena, whose sympathetic spirit at once saw that he was ill at ease.

"Because I do not see how he is to gain his bread," replied the Rector; "and I do not believe he has the means of gaining shelter even for a single night."

"You cannot be quite sure of that, Edward," said Mrs. Carlton; "I have some little faith in his prudence. I do not think he would have thrown himself upon the world in an utterly destitute condition."

"And, remember, he knows the resources of London perfectly well," said Lena; "then he is so clever, I daresay he will manage to get on somehow."

"For my part, I envy him," said Grace. "That is the best of being a man; he has got the whole world before him, and he can go which way he pleases. There is no restraint upon him; he can seek his fortune where he likes, and live, as the birds do, on what chance sends him."

"You talk like a silly thoughtless girl," said the Rector, with as near an approach to anger as he ever used towards his daughters. "God provides for the birds, but he makes no provision for idle improvident men. They must labour for their own life and honour, or starve, or—sin," the last word fell almost in a whisper from his lips.

"When things are at the worst, they say, they are sure to improve," said Mrs. Carlton. "Now that he has thrown himself on his own resources, and knows you will do nothing more——"

"I never told him I would do nothing more," said the Rector quickly; "indeed, I was quite willing to give him another trial."

"Then so much more credit is due to him for not trespassing on your generosity. He felt you had been tried far enough, and has chosen to throw himself on his own resources. I feel confident he will do well. Adversity brings out many virtues, and—hark! what's that?"

There was some one tapping impatiently at the window, and a soft pleading voice exclaimed,

"Let me in!—let me in!"

Mrs. Carlton recognised the voice at once; she opened the shutters, threw back the window, and Adrienne stepped shivering into the room. They looked at her in mute amazement. She was drenched through, and the rain dripped from her as she stood.

The girls welcomed her with surprise. Mrs. Carlton speedily relieved her of her garden hat and cloak, while her husband placed a chair by the fireside, and commenced chafing her hands, which were cold and blue from the unusual exposure. For some moments she remained silently submitting to their kind attentions, not appearing to hear their voices. At last she clasped the Rector's hand with both her own, and said, with an accent of profound grief,

"Oh! Mr. Carlton, let me stay here; pray do not send me home again!"

"We will talk of that presently," he replied kindly. "You must compose yourself; at present you seem too agitated even to think calmly."

Of course they were all amazed, and well aware that some unusual chance had sent Adrienne there at such an hour, and in such a state. But they asked her no questions, and paid no heed to the incoherent words she uttered, as they united their efforts to comfort her. As soon as he could do so unobserved, Mr. Carlton withdrew his daughters from the room, and left Adrienne to his wife's care, feeling that she was best able to deal with the young girl's trouble, in whatever shape it had fallen upon her.

Left alone with Adrienne, Mrs. Carlton used all her soothing powers to quiet and subdue the overwhelming excitement that agitated her. Under such tender influence the feverish glitter faded from her eyes; their flashing light was quenched in a flood of tears. Mrs. Carlton let them flow on uninterruptedly; in a few moments they trickled slowly down her cheeks, as she leaned with closed eyes on Mrs. Carlton's breast. For a brief space she allowed her to remain thus, then she said—

"There, you are more yourself now, Adrienne, are you not? Now you may speak—tell me what is the matter? What has happened to distress you so sadly? Is anything wrong at home?"

"Yes, everything is wrong!" replied Adrienne, lifting her head passionately. "My dog!—my poor dog!—he loved me, and they have killed him!"

Then the wild, impulsive heart poured out the story of its follies and its wrongs to Mrs. Carlton's attentive ear. She was shocked at poor Neptune's fate, but would not express all the abhorrence she felt, as it was her desire to soothe and reconcile, not to incense Adrienne further, who was already bitter enough against her mother.

"It does seem a cruel act," she said, "and I sympathise with you heartily, my poor Adrienne; but, after all, perhaps your mother thought she was doing right. If she thought the dog was dangerous, in her very fears for you she might destroy him."

"No! no!" exclaimed Adrienne, bitterly, "in her unnatural hatred of me she has destroyed him! *I* offended her, and she has wreaked her vengeance, coward-like, on my poor dog. She could reach my heart no other way, so she struck at me through him. But I will never see her face again, Mrs. Carlton—*never!*"

She uttered these words with a concentration of passion that startled Mrs. Carlton, who had seen her often irritated, hurt, and angry, but never in such determined rebellion as now. Every feeling seemed up in arms.

"Hush! remember, Adrienne, she is your mother."

"Why should *I* remember what she has forgotten?" exclaimed Adrienne. "She has never been a mother to me. When I was a little child I felt she hated me. She never kissed or caressed me as other mothers do; often I have crept away into some quiet corner and cried bitterly, wondering why I was born, and what I could do to make her care for me a little. I *have* tried, but she has never changed—she is always the same cold, stern, and loveless mother to me. Sometimes," she added, passionately—"yes, often, I am tired of living, and I wish now that I could lie down by my poor dog and die!"

She burst into a paroxysm of tears. Mrs. Carlton bent over her soothingly, as she said,

"My poor child, I must not hear you talk like this. Matters may be bad between you and your mother; there seems to be no love, no sympathy between you. I will not allow myself to speak of the right or wrong on either side, but you must not brood over your troubles like this, Adrienne," she added, tenderly. "The constant irritation your sensitive spirit feels against your mother, the frequent rising of your rebellious will against hers, will never make matters better. I feel for you deeply, but there is nothing to be done—nothing. My dear child, you must try and school yourself to bear the evil that you cannot cure. Submit yourself wholly, unresistingly, to your mother's will; in time her coldness will pass away—she must, she will reward you."

"Submit!" exclaimed Adrienne, a wild light leaping into her eyes as she spoke. "Submit to her will, when she has killed the only thing that loved me!"

"She did that in a moment of passion, perhaps; and you, who are yourself so passionate, should forgive that," said Mrs. Carlton.

"Her passion is never hot and fiery like mine," exclaimed Adrienne. "It is always calm and calculating, so cold and cruel that it makes my flesh creep. I suppose I am weak and nervous, but at times I am afraid of her," she added, lowering her voice. "I wake up in the night frightened, and I fancy I see her shadow stealing along the wall. Once I screamed out. I thought—but I cannot tell you what I think sometimes." She shuddered and hid her face.

"This is terrible!" said Mrs. Carlton, almost at a loss to know what to do or say. "You must get rid of these fancies, Adrienne, dear. You allow your imagination to run riot, and exaggerate every evil. You magnify your mother into a monster! Cold and stern she may be, and your warm impulsive nature either freezes and hardens beneath her rule, or else bursts forth in a volcano of angry passions, terrible at all times, and in all men, but most terrible in a child. Come, Adrienne, come, do not sob so grievously," she added, putting her arms tenderly round her. "I do not mean to hurt you, but I must speak plainly; if you do not curb your own thoughts, put a check on your own impulsive nature, there is no knowing where it may lead you. God knows," she added, after a pause, as the young girl still lay sobbing bitterly in her arms, "I wish to help you, Adrienne, if I only knew how!"

"You can help me," she answered, subduing her sorrow, and partially releasing herself from Mrs. Carlton's arms; "it was for that I came to you."

"What can I do?"

"Let me stay here!" exclaimed Adrienne, pleadingly; "I will be obedient as a daughter to you, and Lena and Grace, I love them both, will be like sisters to me."

"That is impossible," said Mrs. Carlton, decidedly. "It is madness even to think of it."

"I am more than eighteen now," urged Adrienne; "in three years I shall be rich, and well able then to pay for any expense I may be to you."

"I was not thinking of expense, Adrienne, that is nothing," replied Mrs. Carlton; "if you were poor and friendless, I would not hesitate a moment, I would take you to my heart at once, for we have all learned to love and pity you. But I cannot step between you and your mother; while she lives she is your proper and most natural guardian. I will do anything, everything in my power, to smooth matters, and make peace between you, but I will do nothing to widen the breach—I dare not encourage you to rebel against her authority, though she may use it harshly."

"I understand," replied Adrienne, and there was a haughty bitterness in her manner as she spoke; "if I were to come to you, poor, cold, and hungry, you, in your great charity, would feed and clothe me; but because it is my soul that is naked and shivering before you, craving for that warm sympathetic love which is its natural, necessary food—you reject me—you turn me out to starve or freeze to death."

Her tone deepened to one of passionate upbraiding; but the next moment she flung her arms round Mrs. Carlton's neck, and with a burst of hysterical sobs and murmuring, exclaimed,

"Forgive me if I seem rude and manner-
less—for indeed I hardly know what I say—
but do not send me away—you are the only
friend I have now! If you reject me, there
will be no one so forlorn, so lonely and lost,
as I."

Mrs. Carlton was bewildered. With all her
knowledge of human nature, she was at fault.
She did not know how to deal with so wild,
ungovernable, yet, withal, so tender a nature
as this. Her heart bled for the poor girl,
and yearned over her. She would fain have
clasped her in her arms, and bid her rest
and be at peace; but that she dared not
do. The world rarely takes the trouble to
learn the whole truth of any case; it takes
a one-sided view, not often the brightest, and
judges hastily, sometimes unjustly. Therefore
are its judgments so often reversed, when
time and circumstances have set the matter
clearer before its blind old eyes. Mrs. Carlton felt that her interference might be con-

sidered as an offence in a social point of view; that many might believe she had been actuated by religious motives; the unfortunate difference of faith between Madame de Fontaine and daughter would supply reasonable grounds for such a suspicion. Hence might arise in the parish controversial discussions, which ought not to spring from any act of hers, and which might be injurious to her husband, or draw down censure upon his sacred profession. Cæsar's wife should be above suspicion; and the Church has enough to do to keep itself pure and bright in its own high and holy place, without dabbling with the faith and affairs of those who did not recognise her right.

In the midst of all Mrs. Carlton's sympathy and affection for Adrienne, she was not blind to her faults. She felt that Madame de Fontaine and her daughter were both to blame; not equally, for she laid by far the greater portion upon the mother.

She felt that the head of a family, like the head of a state, is to a great extent responsible for any uprising that is occasioned by mismanagement, or the want of proper care or skill. She saw that it would be a fruitless task to attempt to reason with Adrienne, or try to reconcile her, by soothing means, to return to the Manor House. Her feelings were so violently agitated; her whole soul seemed shaken and thrown into a state of commotion by the cruel fate of poor Nep. It is the last straw that breaks the camel's back. The last act of Madame de Fontaine's seemed to Adrienne the culminating point of her mother's hatred, and it acted on her inflammable nature as a lighted match would on a barrel of gunpowder; it ignited her worst passions, and fired her indignant spirit with a double sense of injury and wrong. Her anger blazed forth for a time, then, having exhausted itself, it sank down into a wail of bitter woe. Her inmost soul seemed to shudder at the thought of returning to that home which created loathing, not love.

Although Mrs. Carlton could not for one moment encourage the idea of retaining Adrienne, yet she felt it would be almost cruel utterly to reject her entreaty, as she clung to her, half hopeful, half despairing. Instead, therefore, of answering directly to the purpose, she placed before her, simply, though forcibly, the consequences which might ensue, not to herself, but to them, should they consent to her remaining at the Rectory. Adrienne's generous spirit revolted from the idea of bringing trouble upon her friends, and, in her dread lest her conduct should cause them any annoyance, she laid aside, for the time, her own distress. Her hands relaxed their hold—their clasp loosened from Mrs. Carlton's neck, and she sank into a seat, exclaiming,

"I see it now—I ought not to have come here at all; but sorrow makes us selfish. In my wild wish to escape from my mother's roof, I thought of nothing, but came straight to you, fancying, like a mad girl as I am, that you would open your arms and hold me tight, and let me be at rest. But I see now," she added, despondingly, " you cannot help me —no one in this wide world can help me. I must act for myself—without friends."

" No—not without friends, Adrienne; we all love you, and would do anything in reason to make you happy."

" Yes," replied Adrienne, with a sweet expression of affectionate gratitude on her face, "I know you care more for me than I deserve; but you are tied down hand and heart by the world's opinion. You cannot—you dare not help me, even if you would; therefore, it is the same thing, I *am* without friends, and I must bear my burthen and fight my battle alone."

" That is spoken like a brave, good girl; bear your burthen patiently, and wrestle with every temptation that tries to lure you from your duty, from your obedience, Adrienne."

The young girl's lip curled scornfully at these words, but Mrs. Carlton was too much occupied with her own thoughts to observe it. Adrienne rose quickly from her desponding attitude, saying,

"If you will give me my hat and cloak, I will go back at once."

"Not alone," said Mrs. Carlton, stretching out her hand to ring the bell; "I will have the horse put to, and my husband shall accompany you back to the Manor-house, and help you to make your peace with Madame de Fontaine."

"There is no need," replied Adrienne, hastily; "she did not know when I left the house—if I return, she will not know I have been absent."

"I am glad of that; for, if she knew of your coming, it would only increase her anger. She would feel doubly incensed against you and against us. How could you leave the house at such an hour, on such a night, and alone, too?"

"I was not alone," said Adrienne, slightly embarrassed; "the stable-boy was with me—we—we brought Nep here between us—he is there now, outside on the lawn." She lifted her eyes timidly, and half tearfully to Mrs. Carlton's face, as she added, "They said 'he was to be thrown into a hole, but I could not bear it. My poor dog—he is more worthy of a grave than many Christians, so I brought him here. I thought Lena would bury him somewhere in the garden; if I know where, he is laid, and that his grave is cared for, I shall not feel that I have quite lost him!"

Her lip quivered as she alluded to her old favourite. Mrs. Carlton was touched by her request, and answered tenderly,

"We will do more than that, Adrienne— we will plant a mound of evergreens over him, and will never pass that way without a thought of you, and a sigh for him."

Adrienne thanked her, with many tears, for this promise of kindness to poor Nep; then slowly and reluctantly prepared to leave. She was too proud, perhaps too generous, to plead her cause farther, since Mrs. Carlton had pointed out to her the evils that might result to them from their indulgence of her wishes.

Mrs. Carlton was nervously anxious for Adrienne to be placed once more in safety beneath her mother's roof. While they waited for the chaise to be brought round, she felt on thorns, lest any word of hers might awaken a fresh outburst of feeling. She talked to Adrienne, and gave her the wisest and best advice. Adrienne listened wearily, and with a pre-occupied expression of face; and though she sometimes answered with a smile, her thoughts seemed far away.

The chaise soon rattled up to the door, and the Rector was prepared to drive her home to the Manor-house. He did not yet know precisely what had brought her there; but seeing a smile upon her face, he fancied she was going away happier than she came, and he was satisfied that all was well.

The girls came rushing down stairs, though it was past midnight, to bid Adrienne good-bye. There was a confidential whispering among them, then a hurried embrace, the Rector lifted her into the chaise, and she was gone.

He drove in silence through the dark lanes; the rain was still falling fast, and the wind drove it in blinding showers in their faces. Short as the distance was between the Rectory and the Manor-house, it seemed interminable to Mr. Carlton. Once or twice he tried to enliven the journey by speaking cheerily to Adrienne; but she made no response—his attempt failed —she hardly seemed to hear him; she was buried in some profound absorbing thought. Once a heavy sigh, or rather sob, escaped her, but that was all—she gave no other sign of life.

Arrived at the Manor-house, they found the stable-boy, who had hurried home, patiently waiting his young mistress's return. Through his aid, Adrienne re-entered the house, and regained her own room unobserved. A light shown in her window was to be a signal to Mr. Carlton that all was well, and that her absence from home had never been discovered. He waited to be assured of this, and then hastened back to the Rectory.

CHAPTER X.

GOOD AND BAD NEWS.

" We sit by the household fire,
This winter's night in England,
Each life looking out for its own love-star!
Holding our hearts, like beacons, up higher,
For those who are fighting afar."

THE dark tempestuous night was followed by a bright morning. The village was astir early; all things and people seemed to glory in the sunshine, which at that season could be of brief duration. The labourers went whistling cheerfully to their work, ploughing and preparing the ground for the winter crops. Lena and Grace Carlton were up and out in the garden soon after sunrise, choosing a grave for poor Nep.

Before the day was over, they had buried him beneath the graceful boughs of a silver-rinded birch. They were full of wondering surmises about Adrienne, and anxious to know how matters were progressing with her at the Manor-house. Mrs. Carlton waited patiently till the post came in, then she purposed paying a visit to Madame de Fontaine, in order, either directly or indirectly, to smooth matters for Adrienne. She determined to take any advantage chance afforded her to carry out her kind intentions; she could not of course intrude her opinions, or attempt unasked to interfere between mother and daughter in their unfortunate family dissensions; but she intended, if she could do so discreetly, to invite Adrienne to spend a few weeks at the Rectory. She felt that something must be done for the poor young thing. Life, as it came to her, was intensely melancholy, full of bitterness and disaffection; but still it must be borne. The expression of Adrienne's face, as she had seen it the last night—every look, every word she spoke, was fraught with indignant wrath or terrible mystery, and haunted Mrs. Carlton in the morning. Do what she would, she could not banish Adrienne out of her mind.

In due time the post-bag arrived. They all eagerly surrounded it.

"There's sure to be some news of Archie, for the mail came in last night," said the Rector, as he commenced looking over and sorting the letters.

He was right; there was a letter for Lena. She stretched out her hand to receive it, with flushed cheeks and a beating heart. Her interest in postal arrangements ceased on the spot. She retired to her own room, to read, or rather devour, the contents of that blessed epistle in secret. Despite her eagerness to learn the news it brought her, she did not tear it open the moment she was alone, but sat dallying with her thoughts, as though she wished to prolong the pleasure of anticipation, being satisfied that she held in her own hands the power to gratify it. She looked at the superscription; it was written with his usual bold, fearless hand, so she knew that he was well. She turned it over and over, her trembling fingers eager to tear it open; her eyes longing to trace the characters his hand had written; her heart yearning to receive the message his spirit had sent to hers; still she played with her tender feelings a little longer, as though she wished to be sparing with her treasure, and not over-load herself with the rich rare joy that love had sent her.

She broke the seal at last, and her bright face bent eagerly over the precious epistle, as if she feared the words might fade away before she had caught their full sense and meaning. His written words fell with a strange music on her ears, as she murmured them over and over and over again with her own lips. The sound had a clinging sweetness with it, as though, when it left her lips, it would fain have lingered on her ear, as though loth to be lost, and swallowed up in the silent empty air. He wrote as he would have spoken, if he had been standing by her side. The letter was so like the man, she almost fancied he was near her, and could see his face, and hear his voice.

Captain Dundas was not one to write soft, silly letters, even to the girl he loved. There was a manly tenderness, combined with perfect faith, in every line he wrote; as though the strong heart dictated to the firm hand. He said very little of himself, or of his own personal adventures and experiences. Brave men do not expatiate on their own bravery, nor wise men prate of their own wisdom. He told her they had undergone all the horrors of a siege in its most fearful intensity. Fire, fever, and famine had made sad havock among the brave men who garrisoned the fort.

"At times," he said, "we have been sorely pressed; assailed by fire and sword from without, by disease and hunger within. There have been moments when our stoutest hearts have quailed, not at the sufferings and privations we endured, nor at the dangers we daily faced, but from the apprehensions of what the future might have in store. The dread that, after all we had undergone, we should be compelled to capitulate, to surrender; the fear of that haunted us day and night. What would they say of us in England? Would all our struggles go for nothing? We know how these matters are canvassed over at home; if the most gigantic, almost superhuman efforts, are uncrowned with success, they are merely branded as failures, the sublimity of the attempt is forgotten, and the censorship of the fool begins. It is so easy to talk of what ought to be, or should be, when people are thousands of miles away, ignorant of all circumstances, cognizant only of a fact, without knowing its cause, or foreseeing the result. However, thank God! failure has not attended us so far; we waited patiently, and in the eleventh hour help came to us. You will learn how, and receive all other information, from official sources. And now, as I believe you are more interested in my unworthy self than in the progress of the affairs of war, I must tell you that no worse evil than starvation has overtaken me. I am in a perfectly unmutilated state, I have suffered only from a temporary affection called hunger. The surgeon orders me not to overeat myself, and I own there is need for the caution; it seems such a luxury to have even enough bread to eat. How I long for a glimpse of your sweet face! I often fancy myself back again at Crofton; when I shut my eyes I can see the soft green meadows, half golden with the yellow buttercups and daisies, and hear the pleasant sound of the church bells ringing. Do you remember our last walk through the scented hayfield? It is so refreshing to look back on those sunny hours, such a contrast to the gloomy horrors that surround us here. By-the-bye, darling, you ask me to look after Kitty Davis's son Joe! My poor Lena! if you only knew the absurdity of the request, you would never have made it. There are some thousands of lanky lads, no doubt, named 'Joe,' who have done their duty tolerably well. Some have been shot or cut down, some reserved for future glory; whether that interesting specimen of the genus Joseph, Kitty's son (whom I well remember as an efficient scarecrow in your father's corn-fields), survives or not, I cannot tell."

A little more of tender love for herself, kind messages to her father and to Grace, a satire on the stepmother, and his letter was finished. In a short postscript he inquired—

"How do you get on with that queer French family at the Manor-house? Remember all news of Crofton is interesting to me."

Lena read his letter over and over again, with varying feelings; sorrow, joy, and curiosity sweeping over her spirit by turns. She grieved to hear that he had suffered; then rejoiced that his sufferings were over, that he was well, and could write in his old quaint spirits. She was curious to learn more about him, of his personal adventures and exploits; the world was beginning to talk of him, yet he said nothing of himself; no word of exultation at the fame which he knew was rising round him; nothing of the distinction he expected, or the honours he had nobly won. All of which he knew would be a source of absorbing interest and pride to her. Love is egotistical, and she would have had him egotistical for love's sake. For a second she was a little hurt at the light way in which he spoke of the widow's son; then she was vexed with herself for having troubled him, and annoyed with tiresome old Kitty for prompting her to the act.

She was preparing to go down stairs, to communicate so much as she thought proper of the contents of Archie's letter to her family, when Grace burst into the room, her face beaming with unusual pleasure.

"Here, Lena!—look here!—read this!" and she put *The Times* in her hand, pointing exultingly to one of the leading articles.

Lena trembled as she stretched out her hand to receive it; but a glance at her sister's flushed, excited face, told her there was no ill news to be dreaded. Grace threw her arms round her sister's neck, and kissed her fondly, saying with impatient joy,

"Read, Lena, read!" and Lena did read.

It was one of those stirring articles which circulate the blood through the heart of England, making every pulse beat and quicken throughout the whole land; sending one universal thrill of pride and joy into every corner of the British Empire. It gave a full and vivid account of the defence of ——, awarding to all concerned in that wonderful and heroic resistance, from the highest to the lowest, the just meed of honour due to each. Every man seemed to have been a hero, and to have endured, and struggled, as though the honour of old England depended on *him* alone. One by one they had dropped their arms and yielded, but to no mortal enemy. Death slew them by famine, fever, or by fire. When at last help did come to their rescue, they were reduced to a score or two of living skeletons, who had scarcely strength to march to open the gates to welcome their most welcome friends and deliverers. Never was such huge misery borne with such heroic endurance. Nothing seemed to daunt the heroes; as the living dwindled away, they manned the walls with sentinels of their dead. Truly those besieged walls enclosed a glorious constellation of heroes, unparalleled in the annals of war for their daring bravery, matchless intrepidity, and contempt of danger. One spirit of holy enthusiasm seemed to animate every man; each strove to outdo the other in daring and enduring. The officers went about among the men, inspiriting them in their strength, upholding them in their weakness;

trying to smile and scatter hope around them, when it was lying cold and dead in their own hearts, hoping amid despair. They were all resolved that if they were forced to yield, a silent city of the dead alone should fall into the hands of the enemy. Thus a few score men, by skilful strategy, ceaseless perseverance, and unflinching fortitude, kept a whole army at bay. Foremost among the brave defenders stood the name of Captain Dundas! "His name," so said the leading article, "will be a household word in England."

Lena rapidly ran over every line, until she came to his name—there she stopped—she could go no farther. The words danced before her eyes; she could not see another letter distinctly. Pride, a glorious pride in the man she loved, seemed to rush through her veins, flooding her senses, and blinding her eyes with too much light. "His name would be a household word in England," and so it proved. The news with which his name was so honourably united had already circulated far and wide, travelling from town to town, and from lip to lip, until it had reached the remotest corner of the land. It was carried, as fast as winds and waves could bear it, over the seas; far away to the distant colonies, there to be trumpeted abroad, gladdening and cheering the heart of the exile and wanderer, with "news from home." None but those who have dwelt in strange lands can tell how the heart of the absent yearns towards his native land, rejoicing in its joy, and echoing back every cry of sorrow or of pain. How their hearts exult, and their joy bells ring out, at the news of their country's glory.

"Oh! Grace," exclaimed Lena, as she held the paper fast, "how glorious it must be to have a power like this!—to be able to write such words, and send such news echoing through the land! I wish I knew the man who wrote this. God bless him! whoever he is—he has done justice to Archie!"

" Wait till more and fuller tidings arrive," said Grace. "Some may say he has done more than justice to him, and less than justice to another. You cannot suppose that Archie was the only hero of the company."

"I do *not* suppose it," answered Lena, almost fiercely; "I know they were all brave, all heroic, and justice is done to all—read for yourself— but only one can be singled out for special honour and distinction. Only one can be chosen to wear the laurels that cast a glory over all, and I thank God the choice has fallen upon him."

"Of course we are all glad to hear such good news of Archie, because he belongs to us in a way; but all this stir about him makes me think of Laurie—he is as good, as wise, as brave, and a great deal more agreeable, *I* think, than Archie, yet there's nothing said about him."

"What could be said?" exclaimed Lena, a little irritated. She felt that his name ought not to have been brought in at such a time. "He has done nothing in all his life to deserve either admiration or praise."

She spoke the truth; yet the next moment she was vexed with herself for having spoken at all.

"He would distinguish himself if he had the opportunity," replied Grace; "but all men do not have equal chances."

"All men do not know how to seize, and make the most of an opportunity," replied Lena.

"You need not be so severe on poor Laurie; I daresay he has been very foolish; but then he has suffered for his folly; at any rate, we have no right to be hard upon him."

"I do not wish to be hard on any one, least of all on poor Laurence! It was you who spoke of him, and compared him and his failures with Archie and his successes, as though one had anything to do with the other! But it is always so with you, Grace, whenever you see anyone happy, you seem to love to throw in the apple of discord; in the midst of sunshine, you talk of storms. You cannot even look upon a rose-tree growing, but you suggest there may be a worm in the bud, or canker at the root. In the midst of my sweet you throw in your bitter. I do believe you are jealous of Archie!—of his success, of my pride and glory in him!"

"It is quite natural that I would rather be proud of my brother than of your lover," replied Grace, angrily.

"It is natural we should give honour to those to whom honour is due," said Lena, "be they strangers, or near and dear to us."

"But, Lena——"

"I will not talk of him, nor of anything just now," she answered, impatiently; "please go, Grace, I want to be alone—to thank God for all this good, and pray that I may not go mad with the joy of it."

Grace had never seen her sister so disturbed

and irritated before; had never heard her speak so "unkindly," she called it, of her brother, or so sharply to her. She went down stairs, thinking how horribly selfish and unnatural love had made Lena.

As she re-entered the room, where she had left her father and Mrs. Carlton a few moments back, she found that a visitor had arrived during her absence. Mr. Sterndale was seated there, looking unusually grave, as though some strange accident had happened, to scare away his natural good spirits. The Rector and his wife looked as though a thunderbolt had fallen among them. Grace glanced from one to the other in amazement. She had no time to do more than wonder what had happened, when Mrs. Carlton exclaimed,

"Gone! Adrienne gone! it is impossible!"

"I wish it were," said Mr. Sterndale; "unfortunately it is too true."

"She cannot have got far away—she will be found and brought back."

"No. Madame de Fontaine declares that she will not let a finger stir in search of her. From some words she let fall, I fancy she believes that her daughter has taken refuge here, with you."

"She was here last night," said the Rector; "now I wish she had stayed. I had a presentiment something would go wrong with her."

"At what time did she leave the Rectory?" inquired Mr. Sterndale, eagerly. "I do not believe she ever returned home."

"Yes, she did," replied Mr. Carlton; "my wife had a long talk with her, and I myself drove her back to the Manor-house; it was almost midnight when we arrived there."

"What is to be done?" exclaimed Mrs. Carlton, her distress for Adrienne keeping her silent until now.

"I don't see what can be done," said Mr. Sterndale. "Madame de Fontaine says that, as she went away of her own free will, she must in like manner return, or not at all."

"Something *must* be done," said Mrs. Carlton. "If her mother—her natural protector—will do nothing in the matter, we must. In common Christian charity we cannot let this young girl rush to her ruin, without stretching out a hand to save her. An unprotected girl is so utterly helpless in the world."

"I really do not see my way clearly," said the Rector. "I feel for this poor girl as much as you do, Christina; but I really do not see what we can do—in what way we can help her."

"We must find some way," said Mrs. Carlton.

"It is a very difficult matter, and requires a great deal of consideration—we must not act from impulse, however good that impulse may be."

"Impulse will generally lead us right," urged Mrs. Carlton; "while we may often wander in, out, and around the labyrinth of reason, till we are altogether lost."

"I agree with the Rector," broke in Mr. Sterndale. "If Madame de Fontaine has so little interest in her daughter, that she will make no exertion to reclaim her, I do not exactly see what we can do."

"Reclaim her!" repeated Mrs. Carlton; "you speak as if the poor child had done some great wrong."

"So she has," exclaimed the Rector. "You cannot deny that, Christina. If a girl is to rebel against parental authority, to take offence lightly, and, in a moment of irritation, fly from her home and throw herself upon the world, there is an end of domestic rule; the influence of home is over."

"Things went very hard with her," said Mrs. Carlton. "It was terrible to live in that cold, unsympathising, loveless home, drearily dragging life on from day to day, with no change, no hope even of an end."

"Time ends or changes all things," replied the Rector. "We should bide God's will, and wait."

"She was sorely tried," murmured Mrs. Carlton, as though following the extenuating thoughts that passed through her own mind, rather than answering him.

"Unhappily the days of knight-errantry are past, or I would mount my beast and start in search of her," said Mr. Sterndale. "It is impossible not to feel the deepest interest in a creature so young, so beautiful, and, I must add, so unfortunate."

"Unfortunate indeed!" said Mr. Carlton. "*I* sympathise with the poor child heartily; but I do not see what we can do—we are powerless."

"We are never powerless to do good, unless the will is wanting," answered Mrs. Carlton. "Some expedient must be found. If Madame de Fontaine is so unnatural as to disown her daughter——"

"We cannot interfere," said the Rector hastily. "If her mother is dead to her sense of duty——"

"We must be awake to ours. If she is determined to disown her child—for her indifference is equivalent to disowning—she is doubly an orphan, doubly alone. Her case is one that demands our interference. If you saw a man sinking in the sea, would you let him drown, because *you* were a stranger, and his friends stood by un-caring—unheeding? No! you would plunge in and try to save him. So we must plunge in this sea of misery and try to save this unfortunate girl from her wilful passions, before the waves of the world close over her."

Mrs. Carlton urged and argued her point, until she gained the Rector's permission to make all necessary and possible exertions to discover whither the poor girl's proud, passionate spirit had carried her.

CHAPTER XI.

COULD HE DO OTHERWISE?

" I cannot do it!   Urge me on no more.
He is my kinsman—am I not his heir ?
I would not for the universe his life
One moment rested in my trembling hands,
Lest I might lose it."

TIME passed.   No news of Laurence.   No news of Adrienne.   They had dropt out of the busy little village of Crofton as though their lives had been written on a slate, and wiped out with a sponge.   All attempts to gain intelligence of Adrienne proved unavailing. Mrs. Carlton had carried out her benevolent purpose to the fullest extent, but all her endeavours were frustrated; at last she was obliged to sit down, and wait patiently till

fate or chance brought them face to face again.
They made no attempt to discover Laurence,
or recall him home. The Rector thought of
him for awhile regretfully. Of course he
would rather things had been different; but
what was done and past could not be recalled,
it was beyond help now, and by degrees,
thanks to Mrs. Carlton's cheering influence,
he became reconciled to his son's disappearance, and was content to leave matters in His
hands who sees the end as well as the beginning of all things. If it were His will,
they would be brought to a happy issue; if
not—well—it would still be well. After all,
Laurence was not a boy; he had grown to
man's estate, and as he was wise enough to
see his folly, his wisdom might amend it. So
prayed the father; he too waited till the secrets
of the future should be revealed. Still a cloud
seemed to have fallen over them, and it reached
from the Rectory to the Manor-house. Mrs.
Carlton had called there, but was refused ad-

mission. Madame de Fontaine seemed to resent Adrienne's conduct on the Rector's wife, as though she had prompted and encouraged the wilful girl in her reckless wrong. A whisper was circulated abroad, connecting Adrienne's mysterious disappearance with Laurence's abrupt departure. Mrs. Carlton wrote to Madame de Fontaine, explaining all matters so far as she could, but her letter was returned unopened. Hence all correspondence between the two houses ceased. Life soon resumed its old aspect at the Rectory, and glided along in its ancient grooves. Mrs. Carlton did all she could to vary the dull monotony that makes country life almost insupportable to some active intelligent natures. She entertained liberally at her own house, and visited freely among her neighbours. Under her bright auspices the village of Crofton became unusually gay. She employed herself actively in getting up charade parties and musical meetings. She even went so far as to encourage private theatricals! The literary genius of the county roused itself so far as to make an effort to produce its own drama. The attempt was praiseworthy, though the execution was but tamely carried out. At any rate, the consultations, the readings, and the criticisms created much mirth and laughter, and, in the end, no doubt improved the mind and intellect of the writers. The very attempt at original composition gives an impetus to thought, changes the ideas, and varies the views of life, even if it does nothing more. When one energetic person makes a move in any particular direction, it is astonishing how many rise up and follow; people who would have remained in a dreary, lethargic state to the end of their lives, wake up and find that life has many pleasant phases to show, many novel variations for those who choose to seize them, and are not content with the mere treadmill work of monotonous existence. Mrs. Carlton's example had many followers. Those who were at first scandalized at the idea of the Rector's wife yielding to such follies, were by degrees won over to join in and enjoy them. They had taken the first step from motives of curiosity, and finding the entertainment rather pleasant, and perfectly harmless, their preju-dices died out, and they consented to be amused as well as their neighbours. The girls at the Rectory found time pass more plea-santly than they had ever expected; even Grace Carlton admitted that, after all, a stepmother was better than nothing.

The wild wintry weather came on, and with it a new guest arrived at the Rectory, in the person of Mr. Creswick. He came down quite unexpectedly, and brought with him the son of his deceased friend, a lad about seventeen years old, to whom he was appointed sole guardian. Mrs. Carlton was rejoiced, but by no means surprised to see her brother; she was accustomed to his eccentricities, and knew it was his habit to drop unexpectedly among his friends at all times and seasons, often going away as suddenly as he came. However, he did not leave them long in doubt as to the motive of his visit. It appeared that the young gentleman, Sir Edward Trevor, had always been in delicate health, but during the last few months his symptoms had increased so alarmingly that Mr. Creswick would not allow him to return to Eton after the summer vacation. He placed him under the care of one of the most eminent physicians in London. He found, however, that there was little or no improvement in his health, and that his sufferings, instead of diminishing, merely changed their form. He then had recourse to other physicians; one consultation followed another; each man seemed to differ in some particular from the other, varied the treatment, and changed the *régime;* till, at last, Mr. Creswick grew weary, and lost faith in all, as no two opinions seemed to agree.

Having heard the Rector speak very highly of his friend Sterndale, Mr. Creswick had brought his young charge down to Crofton, to see if the obscure general practitioner could succeed, where his eminent brethren had failed. A fair-haired, gentle lad was Sir Edward Trevor, with large, sensible-looking eyes, that would have been merry, but for the suffering that had sobered, if not saddened their expression. There was a painful contraction of the muscles of his face, especially about the mouth, that made him look older than he really was. He had a slight stoop in the shoulders, and walked with some difficulty, as though he were weary and weak from pain; still, in spite of all, his voice had a true boyish ring in it, and his heart hankered longingly after those healthy athletic sports which tend to make the youth of England brave and strong—such sports, poor boy! he had small chance of ever again enjoying. The Rector, delighted as much at the idea of getting a wealthy patient for his friend as at the confidence Mr. Creswick had shown in his judgment, rushed off to Mr. Sterndale's cottage in great glee. The doctor saw him coming, and came out to meet him at the gate.

"Well," said the Rector, shaking him heartily by the hand, "I always told you there was a good time coming."

"And I never believed you," interrupted Mr. Sterndale.

"I was a true prophet," said the Rector; "it has come at last."

"And I am afraid it will go before I have time to catch it. But, pray, in what form has this good time come?"

"In the form of a rich patient."

"Pshaw!" said Mr. Sterndale audibly.

"A young gentleman, whose disease has baffled some of the best physicians in London; and he has come down here to be cured, I hope, by you."

"Ah!" exclaimed the doctor, now becoming all attention, "a subtle disease, you say?"

"I suppose so, since nobody has been able to find it out."

"That is no proof; we sometimes dive deep in search of that which perhaps after all lies on the surface. But where is my patient?"

"At my house. Mr. Creswick only brought him down last night."

Mr. Sterndale quickly threw on his great-coat, and started with the Rector without a moment's delay, evidently greatly excited, and anxious to commence the attack upon his new patient.

"I shall be really rejoiced," he said, "to have some tangible foe to grapple with; I am heartily sick of this dull, do-nothing life. If it were not for my poor old mother, I would have started off to London long ago, and attached myself to one of the hospitals."

"Well," said the Rector, drily, "I suppose it is very natural, though certainly not humane, for a doctor to lament the healthy state of his neighbourhood."

"It is not that I complain of, but people will send for me when there is nothing the matter with them. One day a woman has a fit of the vapours, and sends for me to cure her; another suffers from a chronic fit of ill-temper; a third worries herself into a positive nervous fever; in each case, if I were to tell the simple truth, that the cure lay more in themselves than in me, I should be voted a blockhead or a fool."

"You can't make the same complaint of your poorer patients," said the Rector; "they at least have no time to encourage nervous disorders."

"Their vices take a different turn," replied Mr. Sterndale with rueful comicality; "they mismanage their lives sadly, and are daily committing some enormity that ought to be put down by act of parliament; only unfortunately there can be no legislation against the prejudices of the poor; they will go on their own way, too often tempting disease till it reaches their very threshold, and even then they will not take the proper means to get rid of it."

"I suppose they consider that a part of your business," said the Rector.

"But they won't even let me do my part of the business honestly. Unless I attack their malady with bushels of pills, and literally flood them with rivers of the most nauseous drugs sanctioned in the Pharmacopœia, they would have no belief in my skill. If I were to give them simple common-sense rules for health and well-being, to prevent the evils they suffer from, I should be drummed out of the village."

"Here we are," said Mr. Carlton, as they reached the Rectory gate. "Now for your patient, Sterndale—I have bragged so much of your skill, that you must not let the poor boy come down here to die."

"Life and death are in God's hands," replied Mr. Sterndale; "but I will do my best, Rector, if only to justify your faith in me. I know I have always your good word, and you know how grateful I am; but I can only repay your kindness back in thanks."

"Pay nothing beforehand—not even gratitude," replied the Rector, as he opened the drawing-room door, and presented Mr. Sterndale to Mr. Creswick.

"Glad to make your acquaintance, Doctor," said Mr. Creswick, cordially extending his hand; "I have heard so much of you from our friend here, that I am inclined to credit you with the concentrated skill of the whole College of Surgeons."

"Pray don't!" exclaimed the Doctor, laughing; "I am afraid the credit would be dishonoured."

"As credit generally is," rejoined Mr. Creswick; with the slightest possible encouragement, he would have mounted his hobby, and dashed off into the realms of moral philosophy, whither his friends could scarcely have followed him, without stumbling at every step, and perhaps in the end they would have got entangled in some subtle argument, whence the exertion of all their reasoning powers would fail to extricate them. The Rector knew his brother-in-law's peculiarity, and, accordingly, suggested that the Doctor had better see his patient at once.

"True," replied Mr. Creswick; "and I hope you will give me a more favourable opinion than the other asses have done."

"Do you judge by the length of their prescriptions, or the length of their ears?" inquired Mr. Sterndale, falling into his quaint humour.

"By neither," replied Mr. Creswick, with his dry smile; "more often by the length of their tongues."

"I am answered," replied Sterndale; "and I think I had better go; another word, and I may prove my right to a place in your category."

He found his patient in the breakfast-room, lying back on a couch, with his eyes closed, and his hands clasped in an attitude of profound attention. On a low stool by his side, sat Lena, with an open book in her lap, her head resting on her hand, as she read to him aloud "Tom Brown's Schooldays." Mr. Sterndale stood for a moment, and contemplated them in silence. It was a pleasant picture, though perhaps tinged with sadness. The bright girl, in the full, rich beauty of ripening womanhood, her cheeks glowing with health, her eyes bright with the perfect joy, love and pride that lay within her soul. She had tried to put it all aside, to forget herself and her own happiness, to concentrate her thoughts upon the book, and modulate her voice, that it might fall pleasantly on the ears of the young invalid, whose thin, attenuated form, and pinched features, contrasted painfully with her fresh, full youth. His voice only had the true boyish ring in it, as he roused himself from his still attitude, and excitedly exclaimed,

"How I love Digges!—dear, fat, lazy old Digges. I wish he had turned, though, and thrashed that Flashman."

"I think he did better," replied Lena; "he made him feel ashamed of himself."

"Not a bit of it—he cowed him for the moment, that's all; you'll see if he don't bully the young ones more than ever, when there's nobody by to take their part—poor little beggars, he knows they can't turn and strike again."

"Why not?" exclaimed Lena; "to my mind a pigmy need not fear to attack a giant, if his cause be good. If I were struck, I would strike again, even if I were killed for it."

"What a pity you are not a boy!" said the boy, admiringly; "what a jolly brick you'd be—you'd have courage enough for anything."

"I!" exclaimed Lena, laughing; "but don't

you think girls have need of courage as well as boys?"

"How can they?—what do they want to be courageous for?"

"Oh! I don't mean that they should be brave after the fashion of you boys—the courage we need is quite another sort."

"Oh! I see, you mean moral courage; but one sort of courage, I think, is the same as another—a fellow who is a coward in one way is a coward in another—but, there, don't talk—please go on," he added, petulantly.

Lena had glanced up and seen Mr. Sterndale; a pleased smile broke over her face as she rose to welcome him. So Sir Edward re-iterated,

"Go on, please."

She answered,

"Not now, Sir Edward, here's——"

"I thought you promised never to call me Sir Edward again," said the boy in a whisper.

"Well, I will try not—but here's the doctor come to see you."

Mr. Sterndale at once came forward to the side of his patient, saying, cheerfully,

"And the doctor will be very sorry if he interrupts any pleasant occupation. Ah! I see!" he added, glancing down at the open book, which Lena had thrown upon the couch. "Here's my old friend, 'Tom Brown.' A capital companion, isn't he?"

The poor boy had almost learnt to hate the name of a doctor; he had suffered so much, had consulted so many, and with such unsatisfactory results, that he had lost all hope of relief, all faith in human skill. He had only consented to see Mr. Sterndale, in order to satisfy Mr. Creswick's anxiety, and had looked forward to the doctor's visit with infinite disgust ; but a breezy cheering influence seemed to surround Mr. Sterndale, which communicated itself to his patient; the first words he spoke found their way to the boy's heart. Instead of the grave, measured, business-like tones of the physician, he seemed to hear the voice of a friend. The easy careless way in which he took up and alluded to "Tom Brown," who was at that moment the reigning hero in the young invalid's eyes, roused his sympathies, and won his interest; in a few minutes, they were engaged in an animated discussion upon the merits of "Tom" and his friends. The invalid boy realised every circumstance, individualized every character, and claimed an intimate acquaintance with every one; as though they had been part and parcel of his brief boy's life. He grew excited, and talked with flushed cheek and eager gestures of the merits of cricket, football, &c., and then launched out on the delight of boating, rowing, and other manly exercises, until he seemed exhausted. After a moment's pause he turned to Mr. Sterndale, and said faintly,

"Seeing me as I am now, you would

hardly think that a year ago I was a capital cricketer; I have helped to bowl out many a fellow years older than I am."

"I dare say," replied the doctor, "and I hope you will live to bowl out many another."

"Do you think I shall?" said the boy, raising himself on his elbow, and looking eagerly in the doctor's face. "If I can, I am to play in the next grand match. Oh! doctor, if you can only patch me up for that, I think I could be content to go home and die."

"But you must cheer up, and never say die," said the doctor, touched by the boy's weary look. "I hope you will live to be a man, and do a man's work nobly yet."

"I don't know; I am always tired, always in pain—and when the frost and snow come, the boys will be out snowballing and skating on the ice; if I am obliged to lie here then, as I am now, I shall wish I was dead."

Mr. Sterndale promised to do his best to restore him to his boyish sports, and then proceeded to try and discover the cause of his suffering. The brave boy submitted patiently to a minute examination.

"Well, doctor," he said at last. "How about the cricket match? Shall I be all right?"

"All right!" echoed Mr. Sterndale, with a grave thoughtful smile, "yes, my poor boy, I hope so."

As he spoke, he laid him tenderly back on his couch, and begged him to rest quiet, while he went to make his report to those who were anxiously waiting below. Mr. Creswick eagerly asked for his opinion.

"Well," he said, "I hardly know how to answer you—whether I should treat you with the reticence of the physician or the openness of a friend."

"Certainly as a friend; I came down here to learn the truth, and if there is 'a worst,' I wish to know it."

"Truly, then, I am afraid it is a bad case;

to speak briefly, and in plain terms, my patient has a tumour growing near the region of the heart——"

"That can surely be dispersed," said Mr. Creswick, interrupting him quickly.

The doctor shook his head.

"But there is certainly some remedy? A tumour is not generally considered incurable?"

"That entirely depends on the circumstances which surround it. At any rate, it is better you should not be deceived. I tell you candidly, I consider this young gentleman's case a very bad one. There is, as you suggest, a remedy, and only one; indeed, I hardly know if I should call it a remedy at all; it is either kill or cure. As the matter stands now, I do not think he can linger on many weeks, perhaps not many days."

"And the remedy?" exclaimed Mr. Creswick, startled by the announcement.

"Is to cut the tumour out, an operation always attended with more than common danger. Even if it be done successfully, he may, or he may not survive."

"You think his case is hopeless now?"

"Utterly."

"And there is no other remedy?"

"None whatever."

"Then, in God's name, let this be tried!"

"I should like you to consider well, and consult the patient himself, before you decide," said Sterndale; "but don't frighten him—put the case to him gently. If he consents, the operation cannot be performed too soon."

Mr. Creswick, though seemingly cold and undemonstrative, was a man of deep feeling; beneath his cool, half cynical manner, there ran a strong undercurrent of sympathy and benevolence. He had that milk of human kindness within him which is so grateful to the afflicted. He was startled out of his usual self-possession, when he ascertained that death had crept so stealthily on, and now stood so near the boy, whom he had learned to love as a son. He was his favourite pupil, on whom he had grafted his pet theories, and sown the good seed in the breast of the boy, and had hoped to reap a rich harvest from the noble works of the man. Had God willed it otherwise? In a few moments he regained his self-composure, and turning to Mr. Sterndale, shook him warmly by the hand, saying,

"I am grateful for the frankness with which you have treated me, Doctor Sterndale. If a thing is to be done, I think it should be done quickly. Give us till to-morrow; then we will decide, and you shall act."

In the morning, at the appointed time, Mr. Sterndale made his appearance. He had left a cloud behind him on the night before; now, in the morning, a spirit of hopefulness seemed to pervade the Rectory. Mr. Creswick had spoken to his ward, who was quite content to place himself in Mr. Sterndale's hands, and was looking forward hopefully to the result. He was prepared to submit himself to the doctor at once. Mr. Sterndale felt, to the fullest extent, the grave responsibility that rested on him; and was glad to find that he had gained the confidence of his patient. He entered the room with a cheerful face and brightening spirits.

"Ah, doctor," said the boy, raising himself up, "I'm glad you have come. You may do what you please with me; though I am only a boy, you will see I can bear pain as bravely as a man."

Mr. Creswick drew Mr. Sterndale aside and said,

"I will retire, for I suppose you will like to be alone with your patient, Doctor?"

"Not exactly," he answered, "though I think your presence would not be advisable; my assistant will be here in ten minutes."

"It will soon be over?" said Mr. Creswick, inquiringly; after a moment's pause he added, in a voice tremulous with emotion, "I commit his life into your hands with perfect reliance, Doctor Sterndale; I have perfect faith in you.

Whatever human skill can do, I am persuaded will be done. I leave the issue of this day's work in God's hands and yours. I have a strong presentiment that all will go well. It will be a great delight to me to take Sir Edward Trevor home to Trevor Manor perfectly restored."

"Sir Edward Trevor of Trevor Manor?" echoed Mr. Sterndale with unfeigned surprise; "did I understand you so?"

"Yes, poor boy, he lost his father about two years back."

"In Switzerland?" inquired Mr. Sterndale, with slight emotion.

"Quite true; he fell from one of the mountains, and was killed," answered Mr. Creswick. "It will be very sad if this poor lad is to die. He has a splendid property in Warwickshire, which I should be sorry to see fall into the hands of the next heir."

"Why?" asked Mr. Sterndale, curtly.

"Because he is a *mauvais sujet,* the misbegotten issue of some low marriage, and I should not like to see a noble property descend to ignoble hands, and go to ruin, as this undoubtedly would, if it came to such an unworthy proprietor. Do, therefore, for God's sake, Doctor Sterndale, try your best to save the dear boy's life, and the property from destruction."

It was with the utmost difficulty that Mr. Sterndale could retain his self-possession while Mr. Creswick was speaking. His first impulse was to lay violent hands upon him, and make him retract every word he had uttered. A moment's reflection, however, convinced him that Mr. Creswick was speaking in ignorance, and that he had not the remotest intention of insulting the person he was addressing. He therefore determined not to make himself known; but he could not refrain from asking him if the statement he had just made was of his own knowledge, or merely hearsay.

" Entirely report."

" I thought so," said Mr. Sterndale.

"Ah! indeed; then perhaps you know something of the matter?"

"Yes, I happen to know tolerably well the next heir, and I will tell you all about him on a more favourable occasion. In the meanwhile, let me assure you that you have been wholly misinformed respecting him."

"You surprise me," said Mr. Creswick; "but this shows me how wrong it is to give utterance to a report the truth of which you are not in a condition to prove. It is very unlike my usual mode of acting; and if I have offended you by speaking lightly of your friend, I trust you will pardon me."

"You have my fullest pardon; but what you have communicated to me, relative to the situation of your ward, renders me unfit to perform such a delicate operation as that the poor boy must undergo. I am very sorry, but you must find some more skilful operator than myself. It requires a steadier hand than mine."

"What do you mean?" exclaimed Mr. Creswick, amazed at his announcement.

"I mean that I have changed my mind."

"That is hardly fair or right, to change so suddenly and at such a time. A moment back you were willing to undertake this case. Have *I* done or *said* anything to offend you?"

"My dear sir, you have done, you have said nothing to *offend* me, but much to deter me from performing this operation. It is, as you have said, *strange*, but it is true—I have changed my mind, and decline to act further in this business."

"But, Mr. Sterndale!" expostulated Mr. Creswick.

"But, sir," replied the doctor, "an operation such as that I contemplated requires a firm hand and a cool brain. At this moment I possess neither—my nerves are shaken; see, my hand trembles like an aspen-leaf."

"You are right," said Mr. Creswick; "I see you are not in a fit state to act at present.

But what is to become of my poor boy? He has taken to you so kindly, and is willing to commit himself to your hands without a particle of fear. He will not have such faith in any other."

"I would have you consult Dr. Forbes," said Mr. Sterndale.

"What's that about Dr. Forbes?" said the boy, who had caught the last words.

"Mr. Sterndale has changed his mind," replied his guardian, with peculiar emphasis, "and refuses to proceed with your case."

"Very well; if he won't, nobody else shall," replied Sir Edward, putting his thin hand out towards him. "You are the only man I could have trusted. I do not know how it was, but my heart warmed to you from the first."

Mr. Sterndale bent tenderly over the poor boy's bed, and passed his hand over his forehead with a soft caressing motion.

"I am the last man in the world in whom you should put your trust, my poor boy. At this moment I can only advise ; I must not act. Do not agitate yourself. I will talk over the matter with Mr. Creswick, and in the end I hope and believe that all will go well with you."

He turned gently away from the bedside, and withdrew with Mr. Creswick into another room. There they remained for some time in earnest conversation. Mr. Creswick evidently thought that some fresh phase in the disease had startled the doctor, which he was loth to communicate, lest he should increase the anxiety already felt by the young invalid's friends. Mr. Creswick was by no means satisfied; he felt he had a right to receive some more absolute reason for Sterndale's unexpected change of conduct than a change of mind. He thought, and justly too, that it was an improper and an unusual occurrence for a doctor to desert his patient in the hour of need. The Rector was equally amazed when he heard what had happened; he knew his friend so well that he felt certain some strong, all-powerful motive had actuated him.

"I am sorry you feel compelled to give up this case, Sterndale," he said—"very sorry; but I have no doubt you have some good reason for your decision, so I shall not attempt to change your resolution, however much I may regret it."

Mr. Sterndale saw that the Rector was hurt and annoyed at his reticence concerning the motive for his unexpected change of purpose. He could not bear to leave his friend dissatisfied with him, nor to lay himself open to an accusation of fickleness or feebleness in a professional point of view. For a moment he was silent, weighing the matter over in his own mind. Presently he spoke out, and said,

"One word, my dear Rector, will convince you that I am, as I have said, the most unfit person to perform this painful and delicate operation."

"Your unfitness is entirely in your own imagination," said the Rector. "I know you so well, that I have a right to retain my own opinion in the matter."

"My unfitness lies in the simple fact that *I* am the offspring of that low marriage which was mentioned just now"—as he spoke he cast what was, to the Rector, an unintelligible glance on Mr. Creswick—"and I am the next heir to the Trevor Manor and Warwickshire property. God knows, I would rather this poor lad should live a hundred years than die; but the only chance of saving his life lies in the successful performance of the operation I recommend. It is, as I have said, a dangerous one. In an ordinary case I should have the nerve to perform it; in this, I have none. If he should die under it," he added, and his voice changed slightly, "in other hands, it would be the patient's frame was unequal to the shock—in mine it might be called a subtle murder."

END OF THE SECOND VOLUME.